Slab

Slab

ON THAT HALLELUJAH DAY
WHEN TIGER & PREACHER MEET

SELAH
SATERSTROM

COFFEE HOUSE PRESS

COPYRIGHT © 2015 Selah Saterstrom

COVER ART, AUTHOR PHOTOGRAPH & COVER DESIGN

© HR Hegnauer

ORIGINAL DRAWINGS © Sommer Browning

BOOK DESIGN © Connie Kuhnz

EPHEMERA & PHOTOGRAPHS COLLECTION OF THE AUTHOR

PRINTED IN CANADA

Coffee House Press books are available to the trade through our
primary distributor, Consortium Book Sales & Distribution, cbsd.com
or (800) 283-3572. For personal orders, catalogs, or other information,
write to: info@coffeehousepress.org. Coffee House Press is a nonprofit
literary publishing house. Support from private foundations,
corporate giving programs, government programs, and generous individuals
helps make the publication of our books possible. We gratefully
acknowledge their support in detail in the back of this book.
Visit us at coffeehousepress.org.

LIBRARY OF CONGRESS CIP INFORMATION

Saterstrom, Selah, 1974–
SLAB : on that hallelujah day when tiger and preacher meet :
a novel / Selah Saterstrom.

pages   cm
ISBN 978-1-56689-395-4
I. Title.
PS3619.A818S58 2015
813'.6—dc23

2014033359

ACKNOWLEDGMENTS

Grateful acknowledgments to the editors of the following publications in which
portions of this work, in various forms, first appeared: *Tarpaulin Sky; Thuggery &
Grace; Forklift, Ohio; Versal; A SH Anthology* (Fact-Simile Editions); *Primal Picnics:
Writers Invent Creation Myths for Their Favorite Foods;* Heide Hatry's *Heads and Tales:
Twenty-Seven Stories and Twenty-Seven Portraits* and *Not a Rose; [C.]: An MLP Stamp
Stories Anthology; Caesura Magazine;* and *Titmouse Magazine.* Additional thanks
to Gleason Bauer, Square Product Theatre, and its producing artistic director,
Emily K. Harrison, who adapted this novel for the stage in the summer of 2014.
10 percent of author proceeds from the sale of this book will go to Casa Libre en la
Solana, with tremendous thanks for their support during the writing of this project.

for Cassidy Holland

in memory of Akilah Oliver and Charles Schleet

and to speak easy in voices delivered from postcards, no one amongst
   us pure
and to ride the two-wheeler to crisscross the storm, a titled vandal
   in long pants
and to be born with a full suit of aces, these things i remember
   in the gilded hour
and to show not fear when faced with thine enemies, a toast in the
   house of friends

—Akilah Oliver

The worst thing about the theater is that it never begins.

This dreadful intermission may be brief or eternal. Who inflicted the hurt (even if he's dead!) or the world for letting it happen. Even if nothing could have stopped it. Now the person may begin to bargain with God. "God, if I do this will you do that?" Then the person will feel numb, like nothing. *Cherried blots jinx mourning and for saint's sake ruby algae on pond plates shed,* she said, that woman with the clipboard, floating. You must simply accept it.

Meanwhile, some spotlights indicate. Between murmurs in the pitch-black pit and *Enter Actor,* a theater has been.

On the stage, knees agape in my dress, I crouch a bit twisted, arms in a kelpish sway.

While waiting, I consider the other productions.

OTHER PRODUCTIONS:

SCENE IN A HOUSE: The filthy kitchenette, Ragù on the backsplash, a broken plastic thing snaked in the sheets, a diesel cloud of tires burning in the yard, father of baby number one, number two, father of baby number three, number four, future baby of a father, a rebel flag, all of this to unconjure. In a single wavy swoop.

SCENE ON A DIRT ROAD: An accident in a cornfield at night and a grown man, screaming. Elsewhere, a suitcase for a doll-child. The suitcase is a specimen dish, the doll-child, a bloom, dropped. An inky scarlet packet popped. More like a *smear on a glass plate.*

SCENE ON A ROOFTOP AMID RISING WATER: "Oh she happened!" Water slapped her mouth until it filled. And then she sank. Eyes open.

Those productions were a lot like this is now, waiting for it to begin.

ACT I: TIGER

~in which~

ACT II: PREACHER

the PLAYERS

Tiger [see HAIR]

———————

Champ [see WORLD OVERSOUL]

———————

Barbara Walters [REPORTS]

———————

Mother Harriet [ARRIVES one hour early]

———————

Preacher [is just A MAN]

———————

ACT I: TIGER

grrrrrroooooowwwllllllll!

ACT I: STAGE NOTES

THE SETTING & BACKSTORY OF OUR ENCHANTING PERFORMANCE.

SEVEN DAYS FLOODED. THINGS IN THE WATER, ETC. THE NUMBER OF MAKING AND UNMAKING THE WORLD. SEVEN TIMES SEVEN TIMES SEVEN TIMES SEVEN. WHICH HAS, IN TURN, REVEALED OUR STAGE: A CONCRETE SLAB, AND ALL AROUND, PILES OF DEBRIS COVERED IN MILKY SOOT, SPONGY IN PLACES, FURRED. ENTER CHAMP. HE CROUCHES IN THE SHADOWS AND WATCHES. MEANWHILE, FORTY-TWO MILES AWAY, PREACHER WANDERS AN ABANDONED BEACH, PREACHING TO DEAD PELICANS (EVENTUALLY HE WILL BRING ONE BACK TO LIFE). ENTER TIGER. SHE WEARS ONLY ONE FLIP-FLOP, JEAN CUTOFFS, AND A TANK TOP THAT READS,

I ♥ GRITS

(GIRLS RAISED IN THE SOUTH)

SHE STANDS CENTER STAGE, LIGHTS A CIGARETTE, AND PUTS ONE HAND ON HER HIP.

◆ SCENE ONE ◆

~in which~

TIGER *Gets Her Name*

Hey, Cindy says. Hey, I say.

Cindy says Hank rigged up a tent in the Dollar Tree parking lot, that at the Dollar Tree, it's a nuthouse.

To heck with that scene, she says. Yeah, I say.
Yeah, she says.

They've moved soldiers into Big City, Cindy says, and you know what that means. Dancing. The word is to meet at the old highway for a pick-up, you know, soldiers, cash, away so long and all, they'll pick us up in a tank, what a picture.

What is it like in Big City?
Dunno, Cindy says.
I've been seeing that smoke blow in, I say.
Yeah, she says, I've seen it too.

THE CROWD AT the club were regulars. The Bayou Trophy Club for Gentleman was a low-ceilinged shack, Schlitz, Pabst. There was among them a Larry, a Harv. Bellied guts pulling tight against polyester, flesh tumbling and bound in a net of stained shirts.

Reno, so named because his mother believed it lucky, owned the Trophy Club. He was tall with long, greasy black hair and a mustache. His common-law wife was Wanda. I liked Wanda a lot. She was twenty years older than Reno and always wanted to know if you wanted some coffee.

Some nights after the club closed, us girls would go to Reno and Wanda's town house and she'd cook omelets and Reno would put on Pink Floyd, and we'd smoke dope out of a real Indian peace pipe. Reno grew pot in his and Wanda's bedroom closet. I liked the unnatural light glowing in the closet and the buzz it made. I told Reno it was the sound of the pot growing. I know, he said, what most people don't know is how spiritual growing pot is.

The money I made at the Trophy was not much, but it was enough for me, Momma, and baby Casey, who lived with us while my sister was off with sonofabitch Ray. Sometimes Momma would bring over lemon squares while us girls were working and she and Wanda would sit at the bar and laugh the deep, hacky laugh of smokers. Baby Casey would be in the car seat beside them sleeping or cooing.

I once heard a TV preacher say, Prepare your mind. After a year and a half at the Trophy, I started preparing mine. I got a library card and read all kinds of stuff. For my birthday, Wanda and the girls went in together and got me a book: *Profound Women*. It had pictures of each of the profound women and a page write-up about why they were so profound.

WELL YOU LOOK about as bored as roadkill, Wanda said. Do you want some coffee?

Sitting at the bar drinking coffee with Wanda, I watched Crystal's act. She was wearing a peach satin teddy. You know, I said to Wanda, Crystal wants us to wear peach satin dresses at her wedding, when she has one someday. Well that will be real nice, Wanda said.

Night after night, me, Crystal, and Cindy, doing the same tricks, wearing the same old shit, dancing for the same guys who would, before leaving, ask about how things were with Momma and the baby, and did Wanda get her alternator fixed.

This was the first lesson my mind prepared me for: boredom can lead to new opportunities.

The profound woman I liked best was Helen Keller. I went to the Salvation Army and found a Holly Hobbie dress and bought a pail from the Ace Hardware. I gave Reno a piece of paper to read for my intro. Sweet Pea, we all know you, he said. Just read it, I said.

Tonight we have a very special visitation from a profound woman from our past. Please welcome Miss Killer to the stage.

I closed my eyes and held out my hands like a mummy, one hand holding the water pail, and stumbled forward. The pole represented the well. I walked around it in circles, as if searching. When Helen made contact with the well, it was a transforming moment because it was when she said something for the first time ever.

To demonstrate this, I slowly backed into the pole/well, then with one hand I swung around it, the other hand still holding the pail. I stepped away from the pole, put down the pail, more swinging. Occasionally I'd take off a piece of clothing and toss it into the pail.

I telepathically communicated to Helen. Helen, I love you. You truly are a profound woman from our past.

The performance ended when, having completed the transformative contact with the pole / well, I arched into a joyous backbend. The music came to a halt. I popped up, raised my bare chest to the audience, arms open. Water, I said.

Wow, Reno said. At the town house, Crystal and Cindy felt inspired to change their acts too. But to what? Crystal said. Well, Wanda said, you could be an Indian princess. The peace pipe was sitting on the kitchen table.

Well, what do you love? I asked. She had a blank look on her face, like she might cry. Listen, I said, everybody loves something, what about that car you told me about? Crystal had a life-changing spiritual experience in a car when she was sixteen. This car spoke to her. It was after a car accident in which she was spared and a voice, seemingly the car's, said to her, Crystal, it is not yet your time.

That Trans Am, Crystal said. Yeah, I said. Be that.

The next week Crystal performed as a Trans Am. She painted black racing stripes down the sides of a red leotard and strutted, revved, and did wheelies on the pole. Cindy decided to be a mailman. Her long-time neighbor/special friend had been one before he died. Wanda said being a mailman would be a positive way to work through grief issues while simultaneously allowing her to perform to "Return to Sender," a song Wanda adored.

Eventually, I was also Florence Nightingale. Under my nurse uniform, I put red tape crosses over my nipples. Wanda dyed my hair red, too, using a new beauty technique that gave stripes of color. Which is how I got my name, Tiger.

I only danced for soldiers once. A ship docked at the base even though it had been decommissioned years before. The soldiers were loud. Their mouths were full of teeth, more than usual.

They've been off fighting, Cindy says, so you know they are down for some dancing.

Fighting Leader's war. Now they are here, close, but we do not know why and we do not know what has happened in Big City or anywhere. Will they come here? I ask. Well, Cindy says, as far as the old highway for the pick-up. Yes, I say, but why not here?

I think about my mother. I found a broken chair and put it against a pile of stuff on the slab. She sits in the broken chair in the heat. Her face twitches. She cannot move her right arm. Her drool drips to her belly and pools. The skin beneath the drool is soft. If I went to Big City I might get food or water, or, what I want most, help. A doctor. Still, I do not want to go. I think I'll pass, I say to Cindy.

I look at Cindy. Her long blond hair with roots just starting to show, the wedge of dirt between her filthy shirt and neck, her exposed stomach, which will never grow a kid because of a botched abortion she had when she was thirteen that was her step-father Daryl's fault. All right then, she says. Before she turns to leave she grabs my hand. We hold hands tight. See you, she says. See you, I say. We hold hands tight. See you, she says. See you, I say. That was the last time I saw Cindy.

◆ SCENE TWO ◆

~in which~

TIGER *Goes to the Dogs*

It is night. Tiger walks the perimeter of the slab peering into thick darkness. She returns to center stage, counts her remaining cigarettes, and lights another.

Around the block from my sister's kind of shitty neighborhood, there was this huge house where some rich people lived. The people had the house built to look like Tara in *Gone with the Wind,* and it looked ridiculous because the surroundings ruined the effect. It turned out that the people who built that house were rednecks who'd won the Louisiana lottery.

The yard guy who worked for these people was found dead, and they said the dogs had done it. The rich people had three rottweilers, and these rich people found the guy in their backyard. The rottweilers had a reputation in the neighborhood. I'd be taking a walk with my sister and we'd pass the rich people's house and see the dogs, and under her breath she'd say, Oh look, it's those dogs, they are really sweet. The dogs had a reputation for being really sweet. Not like other rottweilers that mauled faces off children. Sitting on Reno and Wanda's porch talking about my sister and the dogs while knocking back some beers, Reno said, Shit, that's the thing about intense dogs; you never know when they'll snap and neither do they and it's all one big happy family until the apocalypse explodes in your fucking face. Yes, I said, I guess that's the thing.

People in the neighborhood wanted justice for the yard guy. They wanted those dogs dead. When I'd ask my sister if there was an update on the yard guy situation, she never said, Boy, were we wrong about those dogs. Then one day she told me it wasn't the dogs' fault; turns out yard guy was on meth, and the dogs were trying to rouse him after he'd collapsed. But at that point she couldn't resume the old myth of "those dogs are really sweet," even though it turns out the myth was true.

Then there was that miserable woman in France. A total junkie, she tries to kill herself but just overdoses. Her Labrador tries to wake her from her drug-induced coma and does. She sits, lights a cigarette. Something I can totally identify with. But when she pulls her hand away from her mouth: blood. She looks in the mirror. Her face: gone. That same day another woman tries to kill herself and succeeds. When the mauled woman gets to the hospital, the French doctors have an idea. Something never before attempted. Why don't we take the face off the woman who killed herself and put it on the woman who got her face eaten by a dog while trying to kill herself? How fucked up is that? I swear to God, French people. Anyway, the irony here: the dead woman lives on through her face, and the living woman has to wear the face of a dead woman.

In both of these stories, people first believed dogs were responsible for the atrocious happenings, but in both of these stories, it was the people's own fault for dying or wanting to.

My grandfather once shot a dog. He had to because it was rabid and this was in the country. Not long before my grandfather died, he told me that for years he suffered nightmares in which he relived the moment before he shot the dog. He had thrown a steak and the dog went to fetch it, which is when my grandfather raised his rifle, but right then the dog turned and looked at him. My grandfather was crying, kind of sobbing actually, when he told me this story.

Maybe he thought he disappointed the dog by breaking some code of ethics whereby you do not shoot dogs in the back, even if they are rabid. A couple of days after he told me this story, he shot himself.

Did he break down while telling me the dog story because he knew he would use that gun again? Here's the answer: who knows.

When my grandfather shot himself, he did it on the back porch where we sometimes kept our two dogs. They were small, cheerful dogs. After his death, they went under the porch and wouldn't come out, not even to eat. I spent a week on my belly under that porch trying to comfort them. After, the dogs were given away. One ended up having a happy life and one ended up having a sad life.

I have read two novels that feature dogs as metaphorical themes. Both books were about the heart, our human dog hearts, our breaking heart hearts, and then just getting on with things. I loved those books when I read them because they seemed hopeful.

I once wrote a poem about dogs and when my lover read it, he was beside himself though he didn't know why. Really, there was a bad dog in the poem but it was about this other guy, not my lover, but a guy I had sex with a week before meeting my lover, an experience I failed to mention to my lover as I was so caught up being in love. Much later, when I told my lover about the other guy, he became furious and ended our affair. There were other reasons, of course, but I look back at when my lover read that dog poem and think, Goddamn.

You also see those bumper stickers, the ones that say DOG IS MY COPILOT. Are the people who put these bumper stickers on their cars making fun of God or AA? It is unclear.

When I was a kid I thought *Cujo* was the scariest fucking movie ever. I remember only one scene, the one toward the end where the sweaty mother and wounded kid are in this tiny hatchback piece of shit that of course won't start and Cujo is pounding on the windows, a killing machine.

I was told as a child that a black dog portends death. Years later, when I was working at a 7-Eleven, I'd get night shifts with this guy, Jim, I had a major crush on. Only freaky or drunk people came in late at night, so we would go out back before our shifts and get stoned out of our minds. Then Jim would get the portable jam-box out of his car and bring it into the store, and we'd listen to music, which I didn't know anything about but Jim knew a lot about. One night Jim played the Nick Drake song "Black Eyed Dog," then told me how Nick Drake died right after he wrote that song and that he had unbelievably long fingernails when they found his emaciated body. Jim cranked up the volume and we listened to the song again, and it was like you could hear it all in the brassy edges of Nick Drake's voice. In the middle of the song a college kid came in to buy some condoms. Jim didn't turn down the volume, so the kid had to buy the condoms with "Black Eyed Dog" blaring. It was so great because it was like Jim was giving that kid a sermon or something, like: *You want condoms? Well here you go and "Black Eyed Dog," motherfucker.* Coincidentally this was the first time I thought about marriage as a personal option, seeing Jim toss the condoms at the kid like that. I thought, There are some people I could learn to live with.

After my divorce, when I thought I was losing my mind, Wanda suggested I get a dog. She sounded so optimistic and adamant about the idea, she was so glad she was having it. And I wanted to be glad she was glad, so I lied and said I thought it was a terrific idea.

My sister got a dog "for the kids," meaning deadbeat Ray and baby Casey, and once when we were talking about something I'd written, she said, You never put in the good stuff, only the bad stuff. And the dog was barking in the background and she had to repeat herself three times so that by the last time she was yelling but right then the dog stopped barking so she was just yelling.

The dogs around here make me feel—what?

The smell of this place wires a jaw shut in pulsing electric stitches. A dead body, unattended, will blow up like a sloppy bomb. Whereas it seems like animals decay in brittle ashy shelves after the initial effluvious eruption from soft-tissued guts.

Most of the dogs wander aimlessly, starving. I watched one lie down next to a jumble of broken stuff and a doll's head strangled in Mardi Gras beads. It lay beside these things, took a shit, and died.

So, to answer your question, Barbara Walters,
I'd say dogs do make me think about death.

I like that they have this streak that tries to wake us.
It makes me feel like something is watching out for us
even though dogs often hurt people when they wake them.
But when I think about the dogs around here, I also think
they are competition.

I could go on and on about dogs.

◆ SCENE THREE ◆

~in which~

TIGER *Has a Devil of a Time*

The first documented serial killers in u.s. territory were brothers Micajah and Wiley Harpe, respectively known as Big Harpe and Little Harpe, born in the mid-1760s. As children, the brothers emigrated with their parents from Scotland, settling in North Carolina, and in the years leading to the American War of Independence, the family operated a plantation. The brothers, by that time young men, fought in the war and, as salt is to a wound, they fought as Tories. After the war the brothers did not return to the planting life; instead they descended deeper south. Along the way they kidnapped three women and forced them to be their wives.

Estimations place the brothers responsible for more than forty gruesome murders. Big Harpe was a grimy, looming man. Little Harpe was petite, an ace at quick cuts. Most of their murders involved butcher knives.

Eventually, killing was not enough. So the brothers began to open the corpses. They put things in them.

When finally captured, and very shortly before his death, Big Harpe admitted to a number of murders but said he bore remorse for only one: his own child. He killed it, he said, because its crying annoyed him so. It was his four-month-old daughter, and holding her by the ankles, he bashed her head into a tree. He wasn't sorry about some of his other children, whom he also murdered. They had made travel inefficient, a different matter altogether.

The man who killed Big Harpe drew the blade all the way 'round his neck, cutting deep through the bone until the head fell off. The same manner a butcher would use with an animal. At the time of his death, Big Harpe was thirty-one years old. His body was left to rot in the unchristian wilderness and his head was placed in a bag, the very same the posse carried the corn for their supper in. They boiled Big Harpe's head along with the corn, the flesh peeling from skull, and it is recorded in the journey book that the corn was good.

Later, the posse found the Harpe women. Tied to a tree and all pregnant. When interrogated, they claimed to have not known the men's bad character until it was too late, and so they were declared innocent, though at times they surely were forced to participate in the darkest deeds. One was welcomed back into her father's home because, documents of the time indicate, she was pretty. One tried to be a pioneer. One just died and was buried in a whore cemetery.

Little Harpe eluded capture and navigated dense uncharted bayous, arriving in the Beau Repose territory, where he gave himself a new name.

The Natchez Trace is one of the oldest roads in the United States, and it begins near Beau Repose. An important trade route connecting the Mississippi River to Tennessee, it was a network of narrow animal trails later developed by the Choctaw. In time, trading posts run by whites dotted the 440-mile road and, in addition to merchants, traders, and trappers, traveling preachers used the Natchez Trace, and it was a preacher Little Harpe claimed to be.

The most notorious place in Beau Repose was the red-light district at the Mississippi River's port, a stomping ground for gamblers, outlaws, prostitutes, and northern frontiersmen. But just outside the district, on the Natchez Trace, some unfortunates leaving the saloons and brothels did meet their bloody end and were thus saved by Little Harpe.

After killing his victims on the old Trace road, affectionately referred to by locals as the Devil's Backbone, Little Harpe would drag the bodies through the Devil's Punchbowl, a large and dangerous bayou infested with kudzu-strangling vines. On the other side and once on his estate, he would dismember the corpses and make arrangements from their parts, ornamenting the land around his humble plantation.

Which is where I lived as a small child. Along with my aunts, their ten thousand children, my sister, my mother, and my grandparents; we all lived together in this ruined house. By which time Little Harpe was long dead.

Bolted into the tree where my grandfather installed a tire swing for children, a historical plaque: LITTLE HARPE HANGED HERE. After a posse hung him in 1804, they chopped off his head and stuck it on a pole as a warning in what we considered the front yard, though really it was a pasture opening into the mouth of the Devil's Punchbowl. It was in this house that my grandfather, a respected Pentecostal preacher in his day, had a vision of the devil.

In the vision he was invited to sit at a grand banquet table filled with every delightful food and many other wonders. Its centerpiece: a shiny silver platter, a shank of meat, and a carving knife. This was no pig or cow, but a person, and it was the devil's banquet, all of which my grandfather said to the gentleman seated next to him, who was in fact the devil himself. Indeed, the devil replied. My grandfather said the devil was an elegant man. You could tell he admired the devil for this. Despite the heinous evil underwriting the banquet, it was a well-mannered event.

We all lived together in this house where my grandfather had a vision of the devil because everyone was poor, and when the grown-ups needed us children out of the way, and they always did, they'd tell us to go in the yard and dig for the devil. A lot of time was spent doing this.

Sometimes we felt we were getting close.
We would say, It's getting *hot*.

My first lover worshipped the devil. His name, true story, was Jesús. I never saw him worship the devil, and I do not know what he did with his other devil-worshipping friends. He didn't brag about it or wear black or make any theological points whatsoever. It was just something he told me one day while sitting on his front porch.

He listened to heavy metal and drank beer and smoked shitty joints. He was like all the guys I knew but different because he worshipped the devil and also because he read poetry. I wrote a poem called "The Paupers of Rank." It was terrible, but Jesús encouraged me. He said I should read Robert Frost. The terrible poem I had written was secretly about Jesús, a thinly veiled dedication to his dark loveliness.

He lived with his mom in a janky half-trailer, half-house affair and called his mom by her name, Juanita. Everyone knew Juanita. She worked nights at the Waffle House, where there was always a man, a man alone, a lonely man, drinking cup after cup, talking to Juanita, who was tough and beautiful. Her skin slipped an inch from her lean, sinewy body, pulling her slightly down and forward. Countering the slippage, her sharp hip bones jutted beneath her tight yellow waitress dress.

She was the only person in the world who could have birthed Jesús, and I fantasized that I opened a flower shop and she became the head florist.

Jesús was one of those guys who never wore a shirt during summer. This was when we were stranded at his house with a losing scratch-off lottery ticket and some trail mix. I couldn't look at him directly because he was not wearing a shirt, so I sat near him, stiffly, an unnecessarily philosophic pose, and there he was, lounging. Lounging, he said, was his thing. Me too, I lied. I complimented him on the trail mix seven times. Each time, I wanted to die. I was suddenly some trail mix freak, some freak of nature who cared about trail mix. Exhausted by this dreadfulness, I told him everything. During the night, in his backyard, in a sleeping bag, after I was finally done, he said, I know another way of talking.

But in order for it to work you have to close your eyes and count to ten.

The next morning I thought, If Jesús worships the devil, then so the shit hell satanic fuck what.

I take two things from this story. One, it explains my predisposition for doing it with guys in sleeping bags. Not in a contrived way; it must happen "naturally." And two, behind the freak is the symbol.

Behind the symbol is breath, filling the oracular cavity created by the collarbone when a person's back arches and everything corresponds.

The Paupers of Rank

for Robert Frost (and Jesús)

you are sweaty, covered in dirt with dirt
beneath your nails there is never anything
in your pockets and you are never up to any good you
with greasy hair with messed up hair
shitty homemade tattoos, dents, the exact scratch
hatching vertical across the collarbone: uneducated,
breathing, formed, raw: the exact scratch. Shining.
Eye level to the gut, the bit under and above the navel,
the marbled layers, that place on a body, and the skin, how
it holds a man inside his body dirt beneath and covered in
dirt with dirt that place on a body, it is true.
I want to be alone with you in a swimming pool at night.
I want to follow you to the ditch. I want you to show me
what is behind the old house.

My first memory of the devil is from church. Pastor Dale was talking about hell and managed to use the word "flush" three times.

I put together the two in my mind: the devil and flushing, something you do with a toilet, and could see this terrible juxtaposition was about to give Pastor Dale a heart attack, so red faced and sweaty he was, and then no sounds came out of Pastor Dale's mouth and his face morphed into a terrible cartoon pig, Porky Pig, whom I feared. And then cool darkness and my grandmother's voice saying my name and that I had 100 percent fainted.

That night in bed I told my sister I had seen a Porky Pig face in Pastor Dale. Yeah, she said, the devil always comes through as a pig. In *The Amityville Horror* the devil was a pig named Jodie, and once, Trudy and her cousin were taping themselves singing an Olivia Newton-John song and when they played the tape back they heard a pig snorting.

What did it sound like? I asked.

Like a devil pig, she said. Like an insane pig snorting in hell.

My cousins and I played games. We played Boat Disaster, in which the couch was a boat and half of us were on it trying to sort out survival and the other half were sharks who had to pull the people on the boat overboard and eat them. We played Honky-Tonk, in which we put mud water in beer cans that we found at the levee and drank them. We held the Cousin Olympics, in which we had events such as Who Can Make Boys Look Like Real Girls the Best.

I also had private games: Dolly Floats Around the Room, in which I would put a doll in the middle of the bed and concentrate in hopes of making it float around the room, and Talks to God, in which I would get in the backseat of my grandmother's parked red Dodge Charger and have private meetings with God.

I would curl into the fetal position, cramming myself on the floorboard behind the front passenger seat. Then I would close my eyes.

Eventually a door would appear in my mind and I would open it. Inside was a dark room with God, who looked like Mr. Roper from *Three's Company* but with jet-black hair. Also, God wore a black suit, a black shirt, and a shiny black tie. It was always the same scenario: God in the dark room, sitting on a Viking-themed wooden throne.

I remember only snippets of conversations during these visits. In one, God said that inside my body there was a very tiny version of myself and as this tiny version I could walk through my veins. Once, God talked about something he referred to as "the shit caves."

Years later I would tell Ricky about God and the shit caves. It was maybe our third date and he had brought a catfish po'boy to the Trophy Club and we were having an impromptu picnic in the parking lot during my break.

Damn babe, Ricky said. That God sounds more like a vampire. You know, at least in the fashion department.

I know, I said. You'd think God wouldn't be so goth.

Hell, he said, maybe that wasn't God you were talking to. Maybe it was the devil pretending to be God.

Well, I said, I guess that would explain the shit caves.

Then Ricky said, You are not like other girls.

It distressed me that Ricky thought I was not like other girls. I only wanted to be like other girls. I did not want to be how I was: a stripper who worked in what could only be called a "sub-genre" way. Then I saw myself outside myself: a woman sitting in a hot parking lot, picnicking on a crocheted blanket, dressed like Maria from *The Sound of Music*. I couldn't finish my lunch. I did not want to be how I was.

When I remember this memory, this is how I enter: through the screen door.

Into the wide fox-trot hallway, therein my grandmother's mahogany sideboard crowded with prayer candles and pictures of ancestors. There are always crepe myrtle petals, blown in from the street, mixing with the dust on the hardwood floors.

Down the hallway, into the den, a ratty couch, a television, my grandfather's old leather chair and my grandmother's turquoise Sears recliner. Between them, a round wooden table with its unchanging items: a Bible, a *TV Guide,* a collection of crystal animal figurines, a framed photograph of my grandparents standing outside their storefront church in Slaughter, Louisiana, 1949.

I like to stand at this screen door in my memory. At this door, I also remember that it was 102 degrees that day and I had been to the library.

It was my goal to read all thirty-three of the *Mysteries of the Unknown* Time-Life series books, of which, on that day, I had read *Mind Over Matter, Phantom Encounters, Psychic Powers,* and *Visions and Prophecies.* That day, I entered the house and plopped my latest stack on the couch and stood directly in front of the window-unit air conditioner.

My grandfather was sitting in his old chair, slicing an apple with his pocketknife. What are we on to now? he asked.

Utopian Visions, Time and Space, and *Spirit Summonings,* I said.

Then we had the conversation we had many times, in which we asked one another if we really believed in life after death. We both always did. This conversation was followed by renewing our vow, in which it was agreed that whomever died first would contact the other still-living person with some feedback. This might occur soon after death, as the soul would likely be ferreted away to heaven or hell, depending.

We never talked about what heaven might be like, only hell, and my grandfather's idea of hell was influenced by Dante. He stood and, in shaky steps, walked toward his bedroom. But at the door, he turned.

Have you been stealing my cigarettes? he asked. No, I lied.

A look of delight came over his face. The look was, you little son of a bitch. Which is what he called his grandchildren when he wanted to refer to them with endearment. But then he said, You know, the deepest pits of hell are reserved for liars and people who take their own lives. Duly noted, sir, I said, and I winked and he winked back.

Standing at the screen door, I remember that day. It was the day before the day I am really remembering and on that day I saw the blood and thought, Who threw animal entrails

on the wall? But behold, an angel appeared. Saying,
That which is conceived is a ghost. Whatsoever shall be
given you, speaks you.

It is not you who speaks.

My dead grandfather was missing half his face, and he put
down the shotgun, lit a cigarette, handed it to me, and said,
I spy something red. That camellia bush, he said, blooming
at the edge of the yard.

Barbara Walters: Fascinating.
Say more. We all want to know.

Tiger: Barbara, I suppose what I'm getting at is this:
the real devil is loneliness.

◆ SCENE FOUR ◆

TIGER *and the*
Glass-Eyed Doll

STAGE NOTE: TIGER THINKS . . .

THE COLOR OF CABBAGE ROT, SLOW AND COLD,
OPAQUE WATER. THE COLOR OF ALL OF US
IF A JUICE, THE WATER. WHAT ARE WE TO DRINK,
GARBAGE WATER. THIS WATER, COLOR
OF DINOSAURS IN TEXTBOOKS, THE COLOR OF
DISEASED, STANDING POND WATER. IT WAS
THE COLOR OF MUD WATER POURED INTO BEER CANS
FOUND AT THE LEVEE, THEN DRUNK AGAIN WHILE
PLAYING PRETEND. STREAKED WITH
THE IRIDESCENCE OF INSECTS AND SLIPPED SHIT,
THE SMELL OF IT AND THE PEPPERED HEAT ABOUT A
DROWNED DOG'S NECK. SWELL OF FLESH SOGGING
OPEN INTO A DE-SHELVING OF MANY MEALY BITS.
THE WATER HAD THINGS IN IT. IF ONLY IT HAD GIN
IN IT. IF ONLY IT HAD TONIC IN IT.

(THE SMELL TURNED HER INSIDE OUT SO THAT SHE
WORE HER STOMACH AROUND HER WAIST AS A BELT
AND THE STORM CREPT INTO HER)

When there is a plan, it is all right. I have a plan. I will get water. I will retrieve it.

Locate water. The water is located. Locate water retriever. Retrievers are abundant in the water and outside of the water, in shapes piled up.

If outside the water, potential retrievers are covered in an ash, a silky powder. It can be feathered onto the tip of a finger, it can silty sash, it can fingertip print. Best to pick a retriever floating in the water. The retriever's only purpose is to gather pure water within the bad.

Pick a retriever, choose one. Surely there is a kettle about. Here is a bucket. There: a gunking hunk, frayed at the edges like torn meat. Many flat screens, floating. There are so many things in the water. For example, that bucket. If I use that bucket, what portion of water shall I gather?

There is this portion here. As high as my hips. But over there it could be different. Perhaps I would not be hip deep in water but on a shelf of earth, and there would be a large item, something that had a function, and it will have a bowl shape in it and within it, good water.

Because of the water I am in, I will swim. But I do not know if the water is deep enough. I could make running motions with my legs and propel myself. But what if there are blades? I have seen flashes of silver in the water. I could construct a raft. It would not be a good raft, I would falter, but it could be enough. Or between its slats, snakes. I have seen seven snakes in the water.

There is also the water of the Gulf. It is in fact the sound water makes: *gulf gulf.* I would like to gather the portion of good water from the water in the Gulf. It will be better than this water or any water near here. The good portion should be gathered there.

I will have to move through this water, into the thickets, until water is as high as my chest. Then swim.

The beach and everything around the beach must be underwater. Imagine a house underwater. A Sears & Roebuck bungalow. The boxwoods turn into wavering kelp. The light is green, the corners dark. It is like any house in any town except the town and its people are underwater. Can the people breathe under the water? Yes. They live in an ordinary way but swim to one another's houses instead.

I will swim toward the *Gulf,* but I will not take this bucket. It is too laborious. I will find a new retriever on the edge of the *Gulf.*

Then I will retrieve good water. I will come back to this exact spot by the rusty ledge. The baby will stay here, curled on the shelf atop. When she wakes, her dull doll eyes will peel back like translucent daisy petals and her other, wet eyes will open. I will give her a drink of the good water.

STAGE NOTE:

THE FABULOUS CARRIAGE OF HER MIND, WHICH
HAS GIVEN HER GRIEF HER ENTIRE LIFE, STILLS.
SHE IS SITTING ON THE SLAB AND THEY ARE CLOSE,
SO THAT IF SHE WANTED, SHE COULD TOUCH THEM.
HER MOTHER AND THE BABY LOOK LIKE THEY ARE
SLEEPING. THAT'S WHAT I'M DOING TOO, TIGER
THINKS, AND SHE ROCKS BACK AND FORTH.

◆ SCENE FIVE ◆

~*in which*~

TIGER *Practices the Art of*
Japanese Flower Arranging

Stealing a car is a crime of opportunity. For example, my cousin Jean Claude knew that every Wednesday, Sweaty Rich Guy would take an extended buffet at Pride Ranch, an all-nude club on the outskirts of Slidell, and that this lunch would last exactly three hours, during which time his red BMW would remain more or less unattended. Because furthermore, Jean Claude knew the bouncer: none other than Dreadlock Dave, who would, years later, become my boyfriend but who, at that moment, worked as a bouncer at an all-nude club and sold low-quality pot.

When stealing a car, the first thing is to jimmy the lock, and if this is not possible, to break a window, in order to gain entry. There are various methods for hot-wiring a car. Of these, by far, the Vietnam Method is most efficient. It does not require you to keep wires together, raise the hood, or even unlock the steering wheel. It requires a flathead screwdriver with an insulated handle and a cordless drill.

At the keyhole, position the drill two-thirds of the way up and drill in about the length of a key. This destroys the lock pins, which allows the switch to be turned on and off without a key. Every pin has two sections followed by a spring, so you have to drill more than once, removing the drill each time in order to allow the bits of lock to fall into place. Next, put the screwdriver in the slit as if it were a key. Then turn.

Luckily, car alarms are so easily set off that most people tune them out. Nonetheless, as soon as you have established the hot-wire, you will have to deal with the alarm. Most alarms are quickly disabled by putting the screwdriver-key in the ignition, turning it forward, and just before the car cranks, counting to five while pressing the valet/override button, found under the dash, until the LED glows solid. The alarm will generally let out a shrill and final chirp, then cease. This entire procedure takes between two and ten minutes, depending on one's skill. It took me three minutes and forty seconds.

Charlie Boy said he learned two useful things in Vietnam: how to roll a joint blindfolded while taking a shit and how to hot-wire any car, anywhere. I once asked my mother what happened to him in Vietnam. She didn't say. She did say that to her knowledge, Charlie Boy had never been forced to roll a joint, blindfolded, while taking a shit.

Charlie Boy lost his keys to the used 1981 Pontiac upon acquisition and promptly taught his children the Vietnam Method so we could drive to the store for beer and cigarettes.

Jean Claude's plan was to lift the BMW and sell it to a chop shop across the river. We would go halves and score some weed from Dreadlock Dave in the process. It is how I first met Dreadlock Dave, and I thought he was sleazy. Still, there was something a little bit wonderful about Dreadlock Dave. The day we got the weed, but before we stole the car, I was fourteen and he ran his hand down my hair to the very small of my back. I could feel my face burning, and then he squeezed my shoulder like a brother and not a brother.

It was this nudie-bar-car-caper gone wrong that landed Jean Claude and me in front of a judge in Saint Tammany Parish, and it is how it came to be that I spent a year in children's prison.

The state juvenile detention reform school was military in concept. On Sundays we went to children's prison church, and the priest was a trembling pasty man who, unsupervised by other adults, did really weird shit during the service. He was crazy, and when I think about it now, it makes me sad. Anyway, classes were held from eight until three. We had a thirty-minute break and from three-thirty until six we attended self-improvement classes, such as Square Dancing.

During my last three months of confinement, I requested and was placed in Flower Arranging. There were five of us in Flower Arranging: four girls and Blake. Blake liked to wear lip gloss, which had earned him more than a few bruises, but in Flower Arranging we would let Blake wear lip gloss. Flower Arranging was taught by Kasumi, which, she told us, was Japanese for *mist*. Kasumi often spoke of Earl. She talked about Earl like we knew him. She was the most beautiful, elegant, and calm person I had ever seen in my entire life, and she is how I came to learn the art of Japanese flower arranging.

We met in the cafeteria. Inside, the smell of sweet corn and bleach, Kasumi cautioned, the words *wabi* and *sabi* do not translate easily.

One translation has it as, "the bloom of time." In order to see true essence, one must look beyond the apparent. Furthermore, she said, three principles govern wabi-sabi. One: all things are impermanent. Two: all things are imperfect. Three: all things are incomplete. Closely associated with the concept of wabi-sabi is, she said (eyes sparkling), Ikebana, the Japanese art of flower arranging.

There are various stories about how the art came to be, Kasumi said, and the most famous of these stories says it began with a violent storm.

After this storm a monk was gathering debris and ruined plants and flowers. Instead of stashing it all in the rubbish heap, he had an idea. He made an arrangement from the trash on the temple altar and sat in front of it. When his superior asked what he was doing, he replied, I am practicing the art of decay appreciation. And so, Kasumi said, Ikebana is translated as "the way of flowers." More than an art, it is a potential path to enlightenment.

The art emphasizes many parts of a flower. Stems, leaves, and wounds are not avoided; rather, they are welcomed as moments of generative energy within the larger arrangement. An arrangement may consist of a minimal number of blooms interspersed among stalks, leaves, absence, and silence. Indeed, while practicing the art, silence is best.

So basically, Kasumi said, Japanese flower arranging is the opposite of Western flower arranging. In the West, flowers are thrown out when they acquire the appearance of death. However, this is exactly when a flower becomes most interesting according to Japanese thought. At the moment of its extinction, the flower is perfect. It is in accordance.

Therefore, Kasumi said, today we can take the Eastern philosophy and mix it with Western culture, and this can give you a unique flower-arranging style of your very own.

At the end of the year Kasumi died because of breast cancer. We weren't allowed to go to her funeral, and the whole day I kept thinking about Kasumi's breasts and wondered how something so slight, because her breasts were very small, could create something so huge and gaping. The night after they took her to the graveyard I dreamed of a deer being disemboweled. This happens after the animal has been hoisted on a hook, and it is the stage between hunting and hacking, and when I looked into the deer's face, it was my face I saw and that is how I feel about Kasumi's death. And even now, right now, I imagine her. You must, she whispers, make more congruent choices. And though I can't see her face, I know her lipstick is blood and her hands are strung with the guts of a chicken, which, Kasumi also whispers, is how the dead perform divination.

Arrangement #13

in *moribana* (slant style) / six cigarettes remaining

Aluminum Foil Bottles Coffee Filters Funnels Gas Can
Hot Plate Propane Pyrex Dish Tubing Clamps Strainer
Trichloroethane Toluene Matches (red phosphorus)
a fema Trailer & some Rubber Gloves

> *The bouquet*: ether-sweet,
> mayonnaise, glass cleaner,
> burnt hair, slaughter feed

✦ SCENE SIX ✦

~in which~

TIGER *Takes Regional*
Favorites to New Heights

Barbara Walters: You've enjoyed a distinguished career as a best-selling author of the mystery series featuring savvy, sexy—at times hilarious—and always smart homicide detective Debbie Python.

Your latest project is quite a departure. *Down-Home Cookin' with Tiger* is already being heralded as a classic among cookbook lovers. Tell me, what inspired you to trade in a pair of handcuffs for a mixing bowl? And when did you know you were not only a chef, but a chef, if you will, of words?

Of all the cakes, I love most red velvet. Barbara, did you know that if a Southern bride serves red velvet cake at her wedding it is considered a slutty thing to do? True story. It's the equivalent of wearing a red dress to a funeral when you have been the mistress of the man in the casket.

The first red velvet cake I ate was made by cake-making Gina. My mother shared a booth with Gina at craft fairs where people also sold things like cakes. My mother's craft was to fashion little people out of dough that she would bake and shellac. These little people were Christmas ornaments. When I ate my first piece of red velvet cake Gina said, That's my son Eddie's favorite too. Well, we should get the kids together, my mother said, and after that Gina and Eddie came to our house and we all ate red velvet cake together and then they came every week and many times Gina would bring red velvet because it was my favorite and also of course the favorite of Eddie, who kissed me when I was five and he was nine.

Days that Eddie would come over, I would make my mother pull my long hair back in a tight, segmented ponytail. A look I despised because I felt it was a "horsey look," but Eddie liked it. On the days Eddie would come over, I would take this yellow paper my mother had a mysterious, endless supply of and, with a black marker, color the yellow paper black so no light came through. I would do this until Eddie walked into the room.

One day Eddie wanted to kiss in a new way and his mouth parted my mouth and his warm tongue was in me. I knew this was not for the faint hearted and was full of transgression. Right before this moment Eddie and I had been having a domestic dispute in the back of the linen closet, a place we often rendezvoused while our mothers drank Budweiser and listened to Willie Nelson. In the closet, Eddie told me about his other girls. I was the youngest and newest addition, but I belonged, Eddie said, to a harem.

Eddie said he liked, on the days he came over, knowing all morning long I was coloring yellow paper black. Why, I asked, did he like it? I don't know, Eddie said, I just do. Then he put his hands on my face and pulled my lips to his, but I pulled away and said, Tell me the names, Eddie. He recited the other girls' names, all seven of them, including my name, in alphabetical order. I was fourth.

Every time we went to the linen closet thereafter, Eddie would instruct me in the new way of kissing. And every time before I would do it, for I loathed doing it and I loved doing it, I would demand that he recite the Girlfriend List. Sometimes I would make him say it twice in a row.

I suppose the Girlfriend List was the first poem I learned. It set up a certain relationship with language, if you know what I mean. From the warm, just-opened space, the heavy light of the body leading to pleasure in the darkness.

Barbara Walters (chuckling): Had it not been for girlfriends and cake . . .

Tiger: Exactly, Barbara.

Barbara Walters: Would you mind sharing some of your delicious recipes for our viewers at home?

Tiger: Not at all.

Red Velvet Classic

Get   a   thorn   from   a   white   rose   bush.
And a box of Betty Crocker red velvet cake mix.
Acquire a jar of gold, magnetic sand. Goat milk, fresh if
you can arrange it, you will need a whole cup. And bowls:
two small, one large, glass, and clear. We shall need a
towel too. Petition that the dram correspond to the nine
conditions, and a bench, chapel length, and a man's bed.
Warm the wax. Form one portion of the halved wax into
the shape of him. Form one portion of the halved wax into
the shape of you. Bake the red velvet cake using
black hen eggs. After it springs from the pan, knife the red,
steaming bread and slip in a dead relative's lock of hair.
Bury the cake in your backyard, under a tree, whole,
with birthday candles on top, burning. Balm, enough to
coat the entire sarcophagus, and wash your slips in blue
water that has within it one pinch of saltpeter. And after
you have done these things, all these goddamned things,
you will be done with it. You will be done.

Barbara Walters: I am reminded of the time I interviewed Julia Child, and she said, "The only time to eat diet food is while you're waiting for the steak to cook."

Tiger: Isn't that the truth, Barbara? I call this next one Icebox Medley, for those times when you have nothing but odds and ends in the deep freeze.

Andouille *ahn-do-ee* vieux carré *voo cray*
French old quarter roux (rue) base of gumbo or stew
lagniappe *lan-yap* boucherie *boo-shuh-ree* boudin chaudin
laissez les bon temps rouler *lay-zay lay bon ton rule-ay*
couche-couche *koosh-koosh* pain perdu *pan-pear-doo*
courtbouillon *coo-boo-yon* étouffée *ay-too-fay* file *fee-lay*
ahn-do-ee vieux carré *voo* French old quarter roux (rue)
base of gumbo or stew lagniappe *lan-yap*
lay bon ton rule-ay let it roll let it roll bayou *by-you*
c'est la vie *say-la-vee* (that's life) mon cher (my dear)
c'est tout *say-too* merci beaucop merci beaucoup

Barbara Walters: How about one more—perhaps a true regional classic?

Tiger: Here's a recipe every Southerner knows.

We   are   traveling   in   the   footsteps
of   those   who've   gone   before
but   we'll   all   be   reunited
on   a   new   and   sunlit   shore
and   when   the   sun   begins   to   shine
when   the   moon   turns   red   with   blood
on   that   hallelujah   day
when   the   trumpet   sounds   the   call
when   the   revelation   comes
when   the   revelation   comes
when   the   rich   go   out   and   work
when   the   air   is   pure   and   clean
when   we   all   have   food   to   eat
when   our   leaders   learn   to   cry
oh   Lord   I   want   to   be   in   that   number
when   the   saints   go   marching   in

◆ SCENE SEVEN ◆

~in which~

TIGER *Hits Shuffle*

Barbara Walters: What do you do for recreation?

Tiger: I like to party with my friends.

I have four friends named Dave. Probably-Not-Gay Dave, Kung-Fu Dave, Was-Hot-Now-Not Dave, and Dreadlock Dave.

Crystal had sex with Probably-Not-Gay Dave and said he was 100 percent not gay, but no one could make the switch to Not-Gay Dave so he is still Probably-Not-Gay Dave.

In the strip mall on Highway 49, Kung-Fu Dave opened a school for kids: Mystical Dragon Kung-Fu. It shut down after a year because kids didn't care.

Was-Hot-Now-Not Dave used to model for McRae's Department Store during an experimental phase when the mall manager suggested all the stores have live mannequins, which made everyone who went to the mall feel weird and sad.

And Dreadlock Dave, who was, at one time, my boyfriend. This was when he was a manager at Circuit City, and he would come to my place after work in his blue Circuit City shirt and khaki pants and drink beer and talk about painting, because that is what he really was, a painter, and then I had to end it because he would not stop wanting to have sex with other women, a lot of them, it was a problem, but by that point we were actual friends so we just stayed friends.

This one time Dreadlock Dave's mom was on some committee with a woman who had a three-year-old son with intense genetic issues. The other thing about this kid was that he had a purple backpack and was very attached to it. Dreadlock Dave's mom said everyone knew about the purple backpack; it was a thing.

The woman told Dreadlock Dave's mom that over the weekend they went to the aquarium and while there the little boy, Ronnie, disappeared. The woman retraced her steps toward the penguin habitat where they had been before. As she did, Ronnie came forward, soaking wet. When the woman asked what the heck happened, Ronnie just laughed. He was all wet so they had to go home. Later Ronnie was playing upstairs in his bedroom so she decided to check on him, and when she opened the door she saw Ronnie playing with an actual penguin.

She phoned the aquarium and said, I think I have one of your penguins. The guy on the other end said, Lady, I doubt that. Well could you please count them, she said, and call if one is missing. Within ten minutes the phone rang, and it was the guy from the aquarium, but this time not so quick and sure. We'll have someone there to get the penguin at once, he said. Can you believe it? the woman asked Dreadlock Dave's mom, Ronnie must have gotten into the penguin pool, gotten the penguin, zipped it up in his backpack, and then it remained undetected the whole drive home. Dreadlock Dave's mom called the house and told me all about it. Jesus, Mary, and Joseph, that little Ronnie not only getting into the penguin pool but getting a penguin too.

Dreadlock Dave and I told that story to a lot of people, and every time we laughed like it was the funniest goddamned thing we had ever heard. Dreadlock Dave's mom did the same thing.

Over a case of beer, we each admitted that it was like we were always waiting for the Ronnie and the Penguin Story to happen, but also like it had already happened. Before we knew each other, before our own births, it is like we knew the Ronnie and the Penguin Story.

I have this other friend, Emily, and when she was in ninth grade, she became completely obsessed with the last of the Romanov Dynasty and it started in English class for gifted kids when they read *Animal Farm* and learned how the book was based on the Bolshevik overthrow of the Romanov Dynasty and that the Bolsheviks were, alas, to prove no less human than the monarchists they had overthrown.

Emily asked for the book *Nicholas and Alexandra* for Christmas and her parents got her the paperback even though they thought it was weird and Emily read the whole thing. She also had her parents rent the movie *Nicholas and Alexandra* and make an illegal VHS copy so she could watch it over and over, which she did. For a while, because Alexandra Romanov and Emily have the same birthday, Emily believed that she was Alexandra Romanov's reincarnation. She loved the movie's score and made a recording by holding a tape recorder to the TV while she watched the movie. And she listened to it every night. She had to write a book report that year and, of course, wrote it on *Nicholas and Alexandra*. Then she had to write a research paper, her first high school research paper, so she decided to write on the last of the Romanovs, focusing specifically on the Anastasia and Alexis question—did they escape? They never found bodies. One of Emily's sources was an episode of *In Search Of . . .* hosted by Leonard Nimoy. Emily's ninth-grade English teacher said that Emily's paper was the best research paper she had read in her entire life.

As a child, my friend Guenevere once gave her soul to the devil. This was while taking a shower and in exchange for a friend's transgressions. After the shower she put on her pajamas and began watching an episode of *Magnum, P.I.* Halfway through the episode she realized she couldn't go through with the deal, so during a commercial, and in a pious way, she crawled behind the couch and recanted.

This one time my friend Noah lived in a house that had old, dented gutters clogged with leaves. This was when he was a kid. There were so many leaves that the gutters couldn't drain; they could only spill water over the sides. Come winter, the water over the sides would become huge icicles, like a row of teeth that surrounded the house. He and his brother would try and knock them down with rocks. Mostly the icicles shattered as they hit the ground. Sometimes pieces were salvageable. Noah took the foot-long tip of one into the house and stuck it in the freezer. Later he tried to eat it but his lips stuck to its surface. What he didn't know: to put his head under the tap and let warm water run. Instead he pulled. When he did, the top layer of his lips' skin remained on the icicle. It looked like a kiss and there was blood all over the place.

This other friend of mine, Terry, somehow managed to crack a smile at the toy trinkets, all sealed snugly within their tough layers of clear molded plastic, dangling from the revolving wire rack. The toy trinkets shimmied whenever someone entered or exited the Kwik-Pak. Although the toys were all presented in the same basic manner, each had a theme. Some said stuff like Spy Kit while others appealed to different interests, like Beauty Queen. Magical Boy was the one that caught Terry's eye. He said this was clearly someone's method of avoiding the hassle of licensing fees and copyright infringement and in that sense was pretty genius—a plastic wand, etc.—all accoutrements belonging to a certain character from a popular series of fantasy books that were in the process of being translated into a string of hit Hollywood films.

I'm not really feeling like a magical boy right now. These were Terry's thoughts. Life felt rudderless. He had done a lot of stuff that summer, mostly drugs, none of it constructive or remarkable in any way.

Also, he was in Alabama and broke. Not even enough for cigarettes. One thing he did have—a late-model T-bird. It wasn't a particularly fancy whip, but he hoped it would get him back to Mississippi, to his beloved crappy futon. This particularly bad day started when he woke in a cold sweat accompanied by a massive headache. He was alone, naked on a foldout, in the garage apartment of a girl he barely knew. He had big holes in his memory. He did, on the other hand, remember chasing a few vials of liquid Valium with tequila.

It had been a big party, considering the tiny size of the girl's apartment. He couldn't stand her rich redneck friends. Terry met Debbie, the girl he barely knew, earlier that year in Big City during Mardi Gras. That experience couldn't have been more different than the one in which he found himself this morning.

The night he met Debbie he was a magical boy and she was a magical girl. They stripped naked and had magical sex on the lawn of the Louisiana Supreme Court as the sun came up. Justice! But then he decided to visit her on her home turf, a mistake. For starters, Terry said, there were too many drugs, too much booze, and too many honkies. Most of the drugs were being supplied by Debbie's guy pal, Tad, who had spent a little time in prison and was making it no secret that he was interested in being more than just a pal to Debbie.

All of these people tolerated Terry because of Debbie, a girl most of them wished they were banging, though in retrospect, Terry said, Debbie was too indie for the boys there but too dumb and spoiled to move somewhere like New York. At least, Terry said, the way New York was before it became overrun with kids who had tons of money but not very many interesting ideas.

Debbie's garage apartment was a few steps away from her parents' house. Not long after Terry woke buck-ass naked on the foldout, he was being driven to downtown Birmingham where his T-bird waited for him in the giant parking lot of Debbie's father's furniture superstore.

Debbie's mother, whom Terry had the pleasure of meeting that very morning, was at the wheel of the large black Mercedes. Debbie sat up front. Terry sat by himself in the back. During the awkward half-hour drive, Terry wondered what he had done that was so over-the-top that no one would speak to him. He also wondered if anything had been done to him, though thankfully there were no signs of foul play. In a few hours he would be in a Kwik-Pak looking at toy trinkets, but in that moment he closed his eyes and listened to the raspy hum of the diesel engine, the only sound, and it was soothing and he wanted, for the first time in a long time, to cry.

This other friend of mine, Frankie, she went swimming in the ocean with her friend Olan, who was a tall, barrel-chested man. Even though the sky was gray and the water rough, they were determined. They held hands and laughed and before long became distracted by some pelicans and then a huge wave crashed down on them and their hands broke apart and Frankie went upside down and her head slammed against the sand and she was underwater a long time. Long enough for her to think she might die. When she finally churned out into the shallows, she was heaving and crying. Then she saw Olan come out of the water, rolling in at first, but then he rolled himself up to his knees and made jazz hands. Even though he was also heaving, he looked at her like, *Hey Sugar, this is the first moment after which we didn't die.* This happened before Olan did die and Frankie was left holding a telephone in an empty room.

Once when my friend Penelope's daughter was twelve months old, her mother-in-law decided it was time for her granddaughter to have ice cream. Penelope, her husband, Ron, their twelve-month-old daughter, and Penelope's mother-in-law went through the drive-thru at the Dairy Queen and her daughter got a small vanilla cone.

Penelope always has her digital camera with her. She says, rolling her eyes, that she has become one of those "scrapbook moms." She has. She documents everything and the first ice cream was no exception.

After Dairy Queen she and Ron took her mother-in-law home, but once there the mother-in-law wanted to copy the ice cream pictures so she could admire them for her own enjoyment. Penelope couldn't blame her because her daughter was the first grandchild and it was her first ice cream and the pictures were super cute. Sure, Penelope and Ron said, so they all went inside the house and Penelope gave her mother-in-law the little blue memory card from the camera and she and Ron headed to the back porch for a smoke since their daughter was sleeping in her car seat in the den.

Penelope's husband, Ron, is a tugboat captain and is often offshore for a month or longer. Penelope wants to be a wonderful and loving wife and to ease the pain will often, well actually quite often, send Ron private photos of herself. These photos, Penelope says, are truly *Hustler* worthy. I'm sure, Penelope says, you get the idea. So she sends Ron these photos and she has a special, blue memory card for these photos that she uses with her digital camera. Not the black, normal one that she uses for all the other pictures she takes.

Penelope and Ron were on about puff five when they realized Penelope had given her mother-in-law the blue memory card instead of the regular black one. Penelope bolted to her mother-in-law's computer room, located in the rear of the house. Ron remained behind, frozen.

Penelope arrived to discover her mother-in-law looking at twenty-five thumbnails on the computer screen, and in terrible slow motion she watched her mother-in-law hit a key on the keyboard, which brought up a picture of her daughter eating ice cream.

How adorable, the mother-in-law said, as she put the images in slideshow mode. Next picture: a full-screen shot of Penelope's Brazilian wax job. Next: a very large fake penis suctioned to a wall, Penelope attached.

Penelope started hitting buttons on the keyboard to make the images go away while accidentally, but still quite violently, swatting her mother-in-law in the face. Finally Penelope threw herself between her mother-in-law and the computer, landing on the desk itself. The brute force of her landing produced a terrible cracking noise from the keyboard, which felt broken beneath her bottom, which she had also managed to painfully scrape. Having landed thus, she found herself face-to-face with her mother-in-law, who stared back at her in silence.

Penelope knew she had to say something, but what? She failed to invent a crisis. She began complimenting the photographs of herself, using language she learned from a Tony Robbins self-improvement infomercial.

The night before the hurricane my friend Emily showed up at my apartment with a bottle of wine and a Vicodin. Apparently two amateur archaeologists had been closely reading the Bolshevik accounts of the evening that the Romanov family was executed.

These people went exploring based on these accounts and found a gravesite containing the remains of two people. Guess who, Emily said, Anastasia and her younger brother Alexis, true story. So they didn't get away, either one of them.

Nobody ever really thought that Alexis got away because he was a hemophiliac but the whole Anastasia thing was a question for almost a century. And now, Emily said, while sawing the Vicodin in half with a butter knife, it's not.

Barbara, I have 386 friends on Facebook.
I have a shitload of friends, and we like to party.

♦ SCENE EIGHT ♦

Some Things a **TIGER** *Knows*

don't look a gift-horse
in the mouth don't shit
where you eat don't upset
the   apple   cart
don't finger your food don't
just   sit   there
don't get your knickers
in   a   twist   don't   let
the doorknob hit you where
the good Lord split you
don't light a cigarette
in   a   meth   lab

♦ SCENE NINE ♦

~in which~

TIGER *Explains the Concept*
Ten Ways from Here to Georgia

You know, Barbara, it was.

It was a career to be proud of. But no height is reached, as you certainly know, without a long journey, and my story is no exception. That long journey is full of good things, very good things, but also many a trial and tribulation.

In contrast to what has been reported, the Trophy Club is where I retired from my career as a performance artist. A career that began many years before, when I was just a girl.

It was in Big City, just across the bridge, where I got my break at the Kitty Kat Klub when I was sixteen years old. I had been at the Kitty for three months when my cousin Anne Marie told me they were hiring at Gentleman's Choice just over in Chalmette, home to young executives, and so I thought I'd make myself some money, but guess what, Barbara? Young executives are the worst tippers of all. They think they should get something for nothing and I made 100 percent of nothing at Gentleman's Choice, but I learned, and in great part thanks to Dixie. Dixie was a real lady of a bartender, and I say, revealing to you now, that she was a man, a man dressed in women's clothing. Now here's the thing about clubs like this, Dixie said one night, all the girls up in here and every joint like this are skinny white bitches.

Barbara, it was true. And in those kinds of clubs, the girls did drugs, a lot of drugs, and I started to see the hustle, how that is what it was, a hustle, and how if you wanted to make money you had to get your hustle together, and this required, in fact, absolute sobriety, which is why, Dixie told me, don't ever drink the champagne in the VIP room.

I couldn't make money at Gentleman's Choice because I wasn't skinny and I guess, aesthetically, it was never a good match. I had too many tattoos, which, Dixie noted, made my look too welfare-slut for the clean-cuts.

Me: Well, I think they'd like that, different from the wife, etc. Dixie: Honey, you thunk wrong. They want something different from wifey but don't want to feel too uncomfortable in the process of objectifying women in an effort to reappropriate their fear of the pussy. Dixie had a theory. In it men feared women's vaginas because they secretly believed they were lined with teeth. You? A big-boned gal that could squash them and don't they know it. What you need to do, Dixie said, is talk to my second cousin Johnny T over at the Five Spot.

Hitherto I believed the Five Spot to be nothing more than a dump: on the edge of Big City, skulking in the burned-out margins, lacking in mirrored ceilings and strobe lights of the Gentleman's Choice variety. Drinking a tall glass of iced tea, sitting across from Johnny T on a Tuesday afternoon, he said, Shit baby, I'll tell you what.

If you got your wits about you, you can pull up to two grand a night on a good weekend. This here is the preferred watering hole for men of business, and you'll do just fine if your head is oriented toward cash and your ass can follow with the enthusiasm I know you got, I can tell by that sassy way.

The thing about places like the Five Spot is that they were, in some ways, more risky than venues like Gentleman's Choice because they were off the grid but on the police pay-off list. The absolutely-no-touching rule, for example, did not apply. Men at the Five Spot were going to touch your ass and that's a fact. But on the plus side, there were cash storms, which never happened at places like Gentleman's Choice. A cash storm is when you are mid-performance and, to show his status, a man will shower cash over your sweaty, gyrating body, all in view of his entourage and all other entourages present. To be sure, Barbara, it was a more physical environment; the distance between you and the men was often only in your mind, which you had to keep focused elsewhere and explains what is called in the business, the "I'm on a beach" look: eyes softly focused on some far horizon, mouth slightly open, a blank look that does not mean pleasure but has come to be equated with that sensation through repetition. Because Barbara, it's about repetition, that's what the hustle is about. And here's a tidbit for your viewers at home: not once did I longingly think of a dick. And neither did any of the girls I knew. Which explains another term in the business, the

"Double-Woot": you keep pulling out those bills and for who? For the girl? No, your friends, that's who, because it makes you a big man who can't be conned by some bitches.

So I'm gonna be up on you.
And take all your money.

A good month for me was five thousand and that's the gospel truth.

The clientele at the Five Spot didn't give a damn about flat stomachs or perky breasts. Meat on bones preferred. Cellulite, c-section scars, stretch marks? Who cares. What we want to know is if you can shake that ass. Ten ways from here to Georgia. If you can shake that ass like it is going to be the death of you.

I moved back home, close to Momma and baby Casey, and started working at the Trophy when Charlie Boy got sick. I don't guess I know what he was sick with. It was the invisible sickness. I guess he was sick with life and death mixed up.

But anyway, that is how it came to be that I lived and died by the stage, alas, retiring from a long and illustrious career as a performance artist.

◆ SCENE TEN ◆

~in which~

TIGER, *as Miss Mississippi,*
Fails to Save Children
or Explain Canadian History,
and Furthermore Confuses
"Whole" with "Hole"

Barbara Walters: Tell us about being Miss Mississippi, Tiger. Most of our viewers may be surprised to learn that a feminist such as yourself was also, at one point, a beauty queen.

Tiger: Don't I know it. These young people today, I swear. They think feminism is a bad word or they don't even know what it means.

Being Miss Mississippi was a dream come true and, in fact, furthered my own feminist concern; that is why I even tried to be Miss Mississippi in the first place. Every Miss Mississippi aligns with a cause during her reign, and mine was gun awareness.

Barbara Walters: It's a pressing issue.

Tiger: There is a saying: You can get the girl out of the South, but you can't get the South out of the girl. And I think it's a little like that with guns.

For example, Barbara, consider Uncle Dwayne. Uncle Dwayne was not my real uncle, but Charlie Boy's buddy from Vietnam days, and when I was a girl, Uncle Dwayne taught all us kids how to load and unload a gun and clean it properly. Then he taught us how to shoot beer cans. Now, I was only seven years old and, as you might know, a Winchester has a kick that can take a shoulder out of a socket if you don't know what you're doing. And you might say, A girl of seven handling a gun? Well, I don't know about all that. Which is exactly what Marion

Horkheim did say to Uncle Dwayne when she happened on us target shooting one Sunday afternoon at Cole's Creek. It so happened that Marion Horkheim was not originally from the South, but from Canada. And so Uncle Dwayne says to her, There is nothing more powerful than the symbol of a defeated nation. By which he may have meant the Confederate flag or he may have meant something else or he may have meant some kind of Uncle Dwayne combo, but what you have to understand, Barbara, is that despite the violence guns expose us to, there is a deep-rooted thinking that guns are necessary, should the people need to take up arms against the government. If Uncle Sam takes away the guns, if he then starts making trouble, who is going to shoot Uncle Sam? In the realm of gun awareness, it's what we call a kind of perfect hermeneutic circle. Now, I don't know a thing about Canadian history, but maybe they have different circles up there, and we may agree or disagree with Uncle Dwayne, but I think it is fairly safe to say that it will be a cold day in hell before guns are outlawed in the United States of America. So during my reign as Miss Mississippi I tried to raise gun safety awareness by visiting with schoolchildren across the state and showing them a darling animation featuring Tommy the Gun, who explains to children what to do if they see a gun, which includes not touching it and telling an adult.

.

Barbara Walters: So, we should say thank you. Not only to darling Tommy the Gun, but also to friend of the family and U.S. veteran hero Dwayne for planting the seed that would lead to your work concerning gun awareness.

Tiger: Actually I credit my gun education a little bit closer to home.

I desired to know how it tasted, so I took a shotgun and unloaded it, the slugs slipping from chamber to palm was satisfying, I heard an in-the-distance sound of horse hooves clopping cobble. I positioned my lips around the flat-black barrel. In my mouth, the gun hole was exact. I sucked and heard a whistle. I heard it in my inner ear. I was curious what it was he tasted. And then I thought, What did he taste like to *it*? The flat-black barrel mouth, a small mouth, how we only ever think of ourselves. Then I imagined how I looked from above: a woman on her knees, a shotgun in her mouth, well dressed, and in expensive shoes.

I took the shotgun out of my mouth and put on lipstick and met the crowd at the crowded place and all night the beer tasted like a beggar's hand, the hand of a person without a home, the filthy hand of a beggar I was licking.

Barbara, when I think of his death, sometimes I do think: Part of him lives in bugs. But also, graphed onto the wall were parts.

What need is there to weep over parts?
The whole of it calls for tears.

Barbara Walters: I am reminded of the time I interviewed Chekhov and he said, One must not put a loaded rifle on the stage if no one is thinking of firing it.

♦ SCENE ELEVEN ♦

~*in which*~

TIGER *Riffs on the Classics:*
Now I Lay Me Down to Sleep

Guardian Soul Mothers

I   am   inside   the   fourth   degree
(do you mind if I smoke for the remainder
of   the   seduction   (Soul   Mothers   I   am   inside
the seduction) I am inside (the fourth degree) watching,
mind if I smoke inside the remainder of the remainder
of the remainder of the seduction) Soul Mothers I am inside
the fourth degree (do you mind if I smoke) watching you
watching me

Soul Mothers blinking in and (out seeking you
Soul Mothers I hate) reject (worship) the slip-gap way
lining detaches from (Soul Mothers You are) will never be
You (want me to) but you don't (want to) want to
Soul Mothers I hate that the foyer is dark I hate pancakes
and I hate suicide I hate this ragdoll sack bloody boy and
I hate the goddamned plot

♦ SCENE TWELVE ♦
~in which~

Tiger *Hears a Who*

The "uncanny valley" is a term from robotics. When a robot is not human enough, it is disappointing, but when it is too human, it is unnerving. The uncanny valley is a phrase that describes this phenomenon.

Yes, I said, that is scary.
We were driving through rural Kansas.

A couple of days before, I had driven to the Mexican border town where Ricky and Suzy lived. Ricky and I made a point to celebrate our wedding anniversary even though we'd been divorced for a while at that point. Suzy ran a brothel under the flimsy auspice of a private club and Ricky kept the property and the books in exchange for a room and outbuilding, which he used for a sculpture studio because that's the kind of guy Ricky was, patching it together with more or less innocuous outlaws. When I arrived, he was halfway through a project in which Suzy would take photographs of the prostitutes and, working from the pictures, Ricky would make sculptures. He had just finished one he called *Hooker Bath*. Suzy laughed while pouring the whiskey. Hell, she said, where I come from we call that a "University of Arizona bath." Suzy had once studied interior decorating at the University of Arizona.

Anyway, Ricky said, that science fiction shit is not about the future, it's about right now.

On either side of the car, endless fields of corn. It was well after midnight. While visiting Ricky and Suzy in Mexico, I got a call from my sister about Charlie Boy. He had not answered the telephone for a couple of weeks and then the telephone was cut off. Unemployed, I decided to drive from Mexico to Beau Repose to check out the situation, and Ricky was along for the ride. We had sixteen hours before hitting the Mississippi border. Ricky passed me the joint. You know what else is scary? I said. Corn.

Yes, he said, agriculture. Agriculture is frightening.

Thus the film, I said.
Yes, he said, thus the film.

Do you know what else is scary? I said. Dolls.
Oh Jesus, he said, hell yeah.

I used to think, I said, the scariest possible line was, *On the way to the county fair there was an accident.*

Yes, he said, I remember. The fragility of the threads that hold it all together.

Yes, I said. It's like everything is fine and then: boom!

Some people are in a car, driving, he said.
They are on a secluded road.

Like this one, I said.
Just like, he said. And then everything flips. There has been a very bad accident.

But what caused the accident?

Something that scampered from the dense woods lining the isolated road, he said, so you know it's not good.

And now the people are utterly alone. Except for the scampering thing, out of view—it was a pin that popped the bubble and led the people deeper into the real doom. They are alone in the sense that they are outside of the recognizable narrative.

Yep, he said, hitting the joint, you got that right.

It seems like, I said, the problem is the accident.
Yes, he said. That's how it seems. But what seems like the problem is really the least of the problems.

And that is scary, I said.
Yes, he said, it is.

THE LIVING ROOM had the usual four walls, but one was made of sliding glass doors. The doors led outside to oil-stained, crumbling concrete chunks. The awning that covered what had been, at one time, a patio, had unhinged and lay as a rusted tangle in the yard. Plumb center in the waist-high grass, a cracked birdbath, two empty Budweiser cans wading in dirty rainwater.

Above the drab couch opposite the sliding glass doors, a picture of a .357. The frame was blue plastic dollar store, the picture cut from a catalog. Above that, a Confederate flag stapled to fake wood paneling. The flag was made of a slick, cheap material.

Left of the couch, a double entry, one door led to a bathroom, one to a bedroom. Right of the couch, a door opened into a small kitchen. Above the kitchen door, a 1970s centerfold secured with a thumbtack. In the picture, a woman wore a fur coat in a field of wheat. She held the coat open, her legs parted. A golden light, a soft focus.

In the kitchen, the icebox was broken. A pancreas-shape of maggots fell from its lower shelf and out of the partially opened door and landed in a succulent plop. Somewhere, a bottle of bleach was uncapped. In its burning work of rendering the rancid smell less, it roasted out that which was most sweet. I turned the kitchen sink faucet knob and cockroaches came out of the spigot. Wings coated and sticky. The wings not gooed together, fluttered. I guessed the water had been cut off for a while.

From the living room you could see into the kitchen. You could also see into the bedroom and bathroom. In the bed, feces in a rut, outlining the shape where a man used to be. In the bathroom, bloody handprints on the mirror.

I keep meaning to clean up the place, Charlie Boy said. He was sitting on the couch wearing a blue T-shirt, naked from the waist down. His hands were shaking from DTs. He ashed in his beard when he inhaled his cigarette.

I have you on a wait-list for the state asylum, I said. They have a treatment program. It's a nine-month wait for a bed. But I have you on the list. The woman at the county clerk's office said it's a really good program.

Well that's just fine, Charlie Boy said.

How did the blood get in the bathroom? I said. There are handprints on the mirror.

Looters, he said. You know how it is up in this poorhouse. Somebody hears something and here they come. I guess they made a mess and tried to wash up before realizing there was no water.

What here is valuable? I asked.
The guns, he said.
Did they get them?
All but the one, he said, and pointed to the .357 in his lap.

Who, Ricky said, are you talking to?
What? I said.

Who?

Don't move, Ricky said, look directly at me. He approached in slow, calculated steps. Do not move. He said it like they say it in the movies.

What's that sound? I said. Keep your eyes on me, he said. What is that sound? I said. Ricky stopped, his hand outstretched. Look at me, he said. I looked down. Blood was seeping between my toes in my flip-flops. What is that sound? I said. Grab my hand, Ricky said. My slick knuckles balled his palm. Don't look behind you, he said. What is behind me? I asked. It is the place, Ricky said, where Charlie Boy used to be.

Is he not there anymore? I asked. He's different now, Ricky said. Why? I asked. He's dead, Ricky said. He's been dead a couple of days, at least. Don't turn around. But I did turn around.

Yellow light through the filthy sliding glass doors, urine light. What is that sound? I said. There is no sound, Ricky said. But there was.

Barbara Walters: Astonishing.

Tiger: Well, I'll tell you, Barbara, it was a little like this: Standing on a hill at night, holding a piece of damaged paper. And letting it go. Watching it disappear into the inky depths of night. And you think, That's not good. You think, There it goes, language.

STAGE NOTE:

If she puts her finger under her tongue and pushes back, she feels an oval-shaped scab. In the moist sanctum, she feels its surface.

She does not know when she will encounter help, much less a doctor. Whatever the issue, it would have to wait.

She pokes with her finger, trying to get a sense of it. And then her finger goes in.

Just its tip. Into a small cavity. The cavity walls have the texture of tongue, firm but spongy. Then she realizes it is a tongue. A small one, and when she extracts her finger from the tiny opening not only does her finger pop out, the tiny tongue does too.

She has no muscle memory of it now or ever and she cannot make it move. The scab lining the opening is itchy. She fingers the ragged scab, then pushes the tongue back into its hole. And it pops out again.

◆ SCENE THIRTEEN ◆
~in which~

TIGER *Draws Some*
Rebel Flags

SLAB

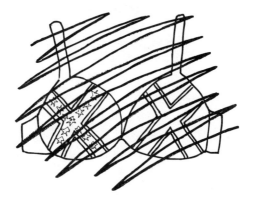

◆ SCENE FOURTEEN ◆

~in which~

Tiger *Writes*

This one starts as a weak man.
In the end, he is so powerful he is a monster.

This one is a wasted life, and, what is more, a slut.
In the end, she has a lovely home and a child who receives a
good education.

This one, Overachiever Jr., despite his alcoholic father,
who he must, at one point, also become. In the end, he
becomes his own man, achieved through his own death,
which he is unable to survive.

This one lacks the most basic metaphysical knowledge and
shoots low in terms of men, who never match her in the
looks department. Nonetheless she gets pregnant. In the end,
she is fabulously extracted.

This one is an ugly loser racked with anxiety and
fried chicken crumbs stuck to his sweating neck.
In the end, he becomes the oracle.

This one, unable to love or be loved, a real cowboy. In the end, he lives in a fake house and is able to be vulnerable with a woman he chooses.

This one, an anorexic, obnoxious, high-strung vegan. In the end, she fucks a Nobel Peace Prize winner.

This one is a mouse in a smock, the type of librarian the public distrusts. In the end, she survives the 1970s.

This one, a typical Oz behind the curtain, a floppy cock behind one-inch velvet plush. In the end, he was a good man and he was a bad man.

This one started sick but died whole.

(this one watched her)

Barbara Walters: And if I might—
this one was called Tiger. But in the end,
she became an actual tiger.

Barbara Walters: The transformation will be complete by morning, a good thing, for if you recall, since this performance began, we have not been alone.

> [CROUCHING IN THE SHADOWS ON THE EDGE
> OF THE SLAB, STAGE RIGHT, IT IS NONE OTHER
> THAN CHAMP.]

Tiger: Do you think he means me harm?
Barbara Walters: I think the more appropriate question is: *Do you believe in life after death?*

Tiger: Why is that the more appropriate question?
Barbara Walters: It is the one, when the theater curtains lifted, you spray-painted on the slab.

Tiger: I must have done so as a way to remind myself of something important, something I would need to know in the future.

◆ SCENE FIFTEEN ◆

~in which~

TIGER *Remembers the Answer*
to the Question

Loot and find out.

She raises the gun she has been holding since this performance began. She aims and shoots Champ in the left thigh.

He had been carrying a makeshift weapon, a piece of board with several protruding nails, and as a result of her aim, it slammed into his right leg, which also revealed a tattoo in a font particular to that place known as the Lower Ninth Ward. A Gin and Punch boy, she thought. Well I should have known. She recalled bars throughout Big City with signs stating, NO GIN AND PUNCH SERVED, attempts to keep out young men associated with this drink, who were also associated with gangs and trouble.

He was bleeding. Please stop, she said. Please stop bleeding. But he did not. Night fell and it was cold. Champ lay still on the slab, occasionally making a strained or gurgling sound, his legs involuntarily jerking. She laid her body next to his and put one arm around him. She touched the side of his head and looked into his open eyes. It will be better, she said, in the morning, I know it will. Shoot me, he said.

< deleted scene >

I cannot get out, though all the mouths of water complain. Champ enclosed and pulled me sore, like a recompense, Champ put his chance against me. He broke my breathing, my portion, for the mouth, in the yoke, through the Lord, he turned a hole inside a poppy that bangs inside the mouth. And the face in your mouth on your face, the pinhole view. The smears cartooned your slit hole with. The articulated clarity of a retained edge, the cresting socket enunioned with the watery-drawn line of your grin. Your swollen honker. Which raises the brow, yet those brows are pinned. Despite the mist that hardly holds, at your most sincere, I see your Roman nose. Below me, my saddle and my love, you who did and did not want more. From the middle, your sex still fountains. Even here? Yes.

When the inner elastic of the architecture snapped, it was madness. It was yours. The slog of the compression does make a sound. So congruent is the overlay that it has become so within.

The hammerblow of the soul mothers bring together what is farthest apart. The spot on the surface, depthing. From the other side you look back at me, in the calligraphic smear of who you were, you collect. Enter me, you say, through my mouth. The blackened hole leaks a dark balloon, your pupils fix. Amen.

◆ SCENE SIXTEEN ◆

~in which~

CHAMP *Thinks It Through*

How unlikely, he thought. But there it was. The sun rose in bland wide bands, and he watched her sleeping form. Sitting on the edge of the slab, smoking cigarettes, watching her and thinking.

After wiping the corners of her mouth free of asphalt bits, she pulled herself up. I dreamed, Tiger said.

In the dream I walked to a café, a place I often went. At the entrance there was an attractive woman. She was laughing, her head arched back, carefree, and I could see my hands moving toward her as if of their own accord. I grabbed her face, a grubby slow digging into the sweet fat of her glistening skin. I felt the danger of derailing into an eternal flux, and then I was angry. I clutched a tight fist full of her hair and pulled it out of her scalp. I brought my face close to hers, as if to kiss her, but instead I stuffed that handful of bloody hair into her mouth and forcefully closed it.

Champ put out his cigarette and extended his hand. Come here, he said. She picked herself up and went and sat down by him. It's time for us to go, he said. There isn't any food or water here so we have to go.

In the distance, sounds of things disengaging from their function. We aren't safe here, he said. He stood and helped her to her feet. They surveyed the ruined scene. He took her hand and stepped off the slab.

After a moment's hesitation, the actress playing Tiger joined him.

I can't sleep, she said. The night was wet and thick, inky, pitch, but a green living shade, teeming. The night's sound was like an oil well: every time the pump lowered into the drum, a hollow boom. The two had been walking a long time, and now they huddled close in a kudzu gulch beside an old animal path. The woman could not sleep because she was afraid.

It was not worse than where she was before, but it was more than where she was before. After they settled in for the remainder of the night, a flying cockroach the size of a crow buzzed past, a wing almost clipping the side of the man's face.

He pulled her closer. Just pretend we are in a garden, he said. Like the time, she said, you told me to pretend the cockroach was a small exotic bird? Exactly, he said. It didn't help, she said. Didn't it? he asked. In truth, it had kind of helped.

It's the Garden of Eden, he said. And we are the last man and woman, she said. You mean, he said, the first.

It made the woman think about marriage; she already knew that story, but she couldn't think of anything else to do. After a long while of sitting there as Adam and Eve, again she became afraid.

How about this, he said, a game. I hate games, she said. This was true. As a youngster she once played a round of Scrabble so intensely that she wept when the game concluded and not, as she was accused of, for being a sore loser. It was overwhelming and suspect to think of each letter having a point-related value.

This game is different, he said. It's called The Metaphysical Postcard Game.

This is how we play. We sit across from one another and close our eyes and wait for postcards to arrive.

They sparkle into existence and arrive in our minds. We can send them back and forth.

What do we do between postcards? she asked. We live, he said. We imagine our lives and we live them.

Close your eyes, he said, and see what happens.

POST CARD

Our passage, each through the other,
illuminates the very limits.

Nature treads the inverse.

A postcard arrives.
If risks were crossroads, I'd pick you.

THIS
CONCLUDES
ACT I

ACT II: PREACHER

Meanwhile, on an Abandoned Beach,
Preacher Preaches

IN THE GARDEN there was a snake.

On his belly let him eat dust, sayeth the Lord. The name *man,* the one formed from the *ground,* his apple, perhaps an inexact translation of "forbidden fruit," commonly believed to be an apple, tappuah haadam, a piece of forbidden fruit commonly believed to be an inexact translation of "a man's throat," and then there was the woman. And the limbless reptile.

Night took the faces of this man and woman and peeled them off like a question formed inside a fetal darkness mouth. There, they saw a blood scene. And when finally underwater, the woman mouthed back, I do. The snake said, Do you want some of this fruit from this terrific tree? She did.

But the true scripture is a scripture of secrets. When you say *dust* you mean that into which living matter does and must decay. Mortal life. But there are older meanings of every word. Dust— breath, storm. Let the storm be in the snake's mouth, let it be his lot and nourishment, he is the creator of reading, he invented nakedness, the Father of the Law, he is the secret that Moses knew.

But before there were sermons:

Little children stitching little stitches hunched over in bad light stitching shut their eyes, puffed guts, the washed-up actress's awful, shaking voice, war, disease, torture, burning-hair taste in the mouth, the blasé attitude of the check-out girl, interstate bypasses, birthdays, ex-lovers, Detroit, Seattle, Brooklyn, heists, fights, putting your hand in and pulling it out, that guy with the camera, that guy with the click-click. Would you like a receipt with that, what about zero percent financing, what about a divorce, and the government, the motherfucking government...

This is what was on Preacher's mind as he crossed Canal Street to catch the 4:15 streetcar. Then something plowed into him and broke his shadow in two.

Born Preacher Broussard in Orleans Parish to a mother, no more than a girl, who named him Preacher in hopes that her son would turn out differently from his father, a pool shark, a ladies' man, a man from Chicago, which is where, the mother of Preacher Broussard imagined, he must have run off to for good after he had his fun with her. It was not to be. Preacher Broussard was not only like his father, but worse.

Lying in Jefferson Davis Memorial Hospital after the accident, almost every bone in his body was broken. He couldn't see out of his right eye and he could not speak, a tube down his throat as it was.

His dead mother paid a visit. She spoke to him telepathically.

Preacher, after my departure, when I first arrived, there was an abandoned gymnasium and within it, chairs. I asked, where are they who sit in these, Lord? Then I recognized my own, a very elaborate chair, I am glad to say, in the shape of a swan. Then an angel said, There are others here, the activity of the sort you'd find in cathedrals between plagues, only, the angel said, you can't see them. All the while I was holding a girl's jewelry box. When I opened it, a miniature ballerina popped up in front of a tiny mirror glued to a turquoise velvet lining. The angel said, Behold, for this jewelry box shall multiply throughout the world. And I saw thousands. I saw them in overgrown fields, in upturned cemeteries, and in abandoned schools. They lined the gutters and hung from trees. They filled a stadium.

Preacher, this is the story of how you became your name.

A miniature ballerina popped up in front of a tiny mirror glued to a turquoise velvet lining and she twirled to the score.

When Preacher was turned out from the hospital, it was Mother Harriet who came to advise him in matters of useful herbs and things. In every neighborhood there is someone who knows the old ways of getting things done. Mother Harriet helped girls in need and read the cards of the mayor's wife. And the local drug dealer's. Because, she said, in the business of fortunes, everyone is equal; you can't be a judge and a card reader. She said so to her daughter, who was learning the family trade. And because of that, Mother Harriet said, her eyes narrowing, you shall never want for work.

She taught the girl other things, too. Such as theater, for Mother Harriet understood its value, that the confession belonging to the mayor's wife was no different from any other's and that the proper environment was encouraging. And another thing, she told the girl, all they ever really want to hear is that they are not bad and can be loved. It is what everyone wants to know; it's the oldest picture show, and it never stops playing, twenty-four hours a day, seven days a week.

These facts never hardened Mother Harriet. They developed her. She often considered the facts while sitting on her porch at sundown having her customary transition-to-evening beverage. During the starling hour, she could hear the ghosts. She was indeed tuned to a very resonant hearing.

Sitting across from Preacher Broussard after his release from the hospital, anointing him and reciting the healing psalms, she could feel how he was a crossed man and then she knew what to do and she did that thing and he wasn't crossed anymore.

Her hands hovering above his wrecked body, she whis-
pered to all the saints in heaven.

> *This body chambrette, this body cadavre contrecoup,*
> *why does this body collapse, when will it wake as new,*
> *this body holds this body, this body rocks this body.*

> *Shadows vanish into this infant body.*

> *This body volunteers.*

When he opened his eyes he said, *In the beginning was the word.* Right off, Mother Harriet thought, quoting the most mystical of the gospels.

Later he would tell Mother Harriet about how, while he was in the limbo place, he saw the way words worked, how each word had a multi-blooming gut that revealed itself as a mass of tendrils reaching down, very deep, as if through the ocean itself, layer by dark layer, until these tendrils exploded into a root ball of ultimate convergence, a holy notion. The cold, luminous fact that everything that is converges into its most opposite expression and then becomes again.

He would tell her about, and together they celebrated, the secret scriptures he learned while in this between place, and she would teach him divination, which is one of the three things a preacher must know.

The other two are healing work and performing sacraments, such as funerals.

NOW LET US talk crucifixion. We know bread feeds people and also that the Lord was a word come down from heaven who was a flesh bread, his corpse eaten and his body remade as our collective body.

Behind the golden curtain in Calvary there is a number, the number 4. Now think about this. What does the number 4 look like? I'll tell you, it's shorthand for the crucifixion, a man hanging upside down with one bent knee. Now take this shape in your mind and watch it turn into a box and what happens when that box opens? The number 5. And behind the golden curtain there is another curtain still, also golden but even more so, and behind it is the meaning of 5. What is the meaning? Change. Change is the meaning.

When Jesus was nailed to the cross, his body outlined that design so perfectly that he became it. Every crossroads has a keeper.

It's not easy to get to the crossroads. You have to be *way* out of town, you have to not know which way to go, you have to be afraid of seeing the thing you are afraid of most, which is seeing the face of the keeper, and all the while you have to know you may not survive seeing his face. Most don't. They die of a heart attack, so intense is his face. Unconstructed and not understanding things only according to their opposite, as he is. Now, at the crossroads you can ask for something but you have to give something. And in your surrender you become the question you've asked and the right path glows and you know which way to go. But don't look back. What you give up, the keeper eats. *How he chooses.*

So when you bring your sorrows to the altar you are on the outer planes of the outer planes, then you fall off the edge. We call this getting saved. Are you ready to be saved today, are you ready to see the true face of the darkest face, are you ready now, I mean are you ready?

The oldest neighborhood was the Vieux Carré and for forever and a day, artists, musicians, and street performers gathered there, and also, on the steps of its cathedral, fortune-tellers. Out of the confessional box into the chair of the fortune-teller. That's how it was. In those old days so many root workers and fortune-tellers were out to trot that the streets smelled like hyssop all the time, which everyone knows is an important ingredient for uncrossing a soul. It was a lifetime ago, Mother Harriet still a girl. She was wearing a light pink dress, layers of sheer fabric in the popular style, for she had her eye on a certain trumpet player she was set to meet, despite her mother's protest, at a quarter past five on a very hot afternoon, a Friday, which everyone knows is the luckiest day of the week for getting paid cash money and being in love. And so excited when she woke that morning knowing all of this and more, much more, that she was standing in the cathedral's square a solid hour early.

With time to kill she decided to get herself a reading about this man, even though she already knew he would, in time, make her pregnant and that eventually she would lose him. That's how it was with trumpet players.

Outside the cathedral, there were many fortune-tellers to choose from, more than usual, as all the traveling carnivals had come to town in preparation for joining up with the biggest carnival of all: Mardi Gras, the great lamentation-celebration. It was a Creole woman who caught

Harriet's eye, the woman's colorful sign adorned with very well-articulated peacock feathers: Madam Surget. Have a seat, Madam Surget said, and that is exactly what she did.

Madam Surget shuffled her cards and laid out two, face-down, across the makeshift table. Young Harriet believed Madam Surget would tell her about the nature of her own heart, which, true, she already pretty much knew, but it was a strange meaning that came through instead.

IN THE SECRET scripture there is also the hidden parable of the man who bent his back.

This man was carrying a mess of sticks. He was going to use these sticks to increase his house. He went to gather them on a Monday morning, but days passed and he was still carrying this mess of sticks. He kept getting sidetracked, so he couldn't set them down.

By the seventh day, the man was so tired he thought he might die. His neck, so exhausted from holding up his head, was now buried in the mess of sticks that had begun to sprout twigs and leaves. The sticks were magical, which is why the man's back was bent. Magical sticks are heavier than most.

And this is the hidden parable in the secret scripture spoken by Jesus when he was only five years old, hardly in his britches, and today I am telling you.

The mess was made of ten sticks and the ten sticks corresponded to ten different kinds of snakes, some as thick as a man's thigh, some skinny and darting. Each snake represented a single life but pictured ten ways.

What the man had to do was put down the sticks and set them free to slither. But the man was afraid. Afraid of losing all his lives and at once. What the man didn't know was that one of the snakes would remain, solidifying into a wooden arrow that could reach any mark. And if the man could recognize the correct target, he would make his mark, his mark fresh as a bright wound, it would bloom in petals of fire, a fire flower, a fire bloom.

The night before, by Preacher's estimation, he had hiked several miles inland. Not once had he seen a standing structure. Now, back on the beach, the early-morning light was dipped in a viscous gauze, hazy, sticky. Preacher moved through the debris, corridors made of ruined parts and exploded subjects, which, in their way, he reckoned, made the shape of water-bloated letters, if one could see them from the sky.

He sat on the gray sand and closed his eyes. When he opened them, they fixed on a pile of knotted driftwood, a pelican's body enjambed in the heap. He rolled up to his knees and scooted toward the pile and dislodged the bird's awkward sand-encrusted weight. He held the pelican's head in his hands. He brought his mouth to the bird's stiff neck and breathed until he could feel the stench and heat from inside his own living form and his lips quivered into words that he mouthed into the bird. The bird's eyes opened. And it took off in flight.

JESUS CAN WALK on water but also, as revealed in the secret scriptures, he has a throne and this throne floats upon the water. There he sits, and the scripture says that to some, it appears not as if he is on a throne atop the water, but rather there appears a water-man rising from water and all around him, the creatures of the water. He can communicate with these creatures and they are known to jump in fanciful, arcing ways.

Meanwhile, in cities, people open their mouths and whistling sounds come out, not even a scream, just pink spit-clotted whines. They want water.

Have you ever been thirsty? I mean *thirsty.*

Do you know where the people can get some water? If you can answer that question, then the Kingdom of Heaven is truly yours.

In fact, the strange meaning that came through the cards could be felt by Madam Surget, who took Harriet's right hand.

She placed it over the first card. Aren't you going to see what it is? Harriet asked. In a minute, Madam Surget said.

Harriet could feel a heat entering her hand. Now, Madam Surget said, close your eyes and tell me what you see.

She saw a town, she saw herself in it, she saw her eyes twitching in light. She saw lives, all the contents disemboweled and mixed up. She saw a wedding veil caught in a tree and a suitcase with a filthy diaper and a washed-out photograph within it, she saw a faded sign for *The Who Woulda Thunk It—Motor Junk-it Grocery* on old beach road. Wherein, she knew Schlitz, a buck for two, and an ashtray by the gambling machine. She saw a beach and everything on it, where a bandit once said, *See my old rattlesnake?* She saw her mother, who was saying, *Run* and *Blessed be the tie that binds.* The man and the rattlesnake and her mother saying it: *The fellowship of kindred minds.* She saw a woman singing, *Delta Dawn, what's that flower you got on, could it be a faded rose of days gone by?* She saw the song and a house in which the song was played, the sadlong kelpish sway, and a ghost who threw a cigar from nowhere into something that was once a room. She saw a postcard: Our hearts are sealed in love. *That was no goddamned rattlesnake!* her mother said. *Almighty chariot fire from above.* She saw sinning and she saw a seashell. She saw a man say to a woman, *Honey, shit, I'll tell you what.* She saw that the sea-lapped hems were moist. She saw a man preaching to a pelican on a heap of trash, *Lord, how I want to be in that number,* she saw that place, slabs, her mother and others too, gone.

When Harriet opened her eyes, Madam Surget was leaning back in her wicker chair, smoking a cigarette with one hand, fanning away flies with the other. Turn it over, she said, gesturing toward the card. And if you do, from this point on, you'll know how to be a card reader too.

This is how card reading was taught in the old days, by what Mother Harriet called "the poetry of disarray." A great and chatty spewing. When she placed her hand on the back of that card so long ago, she saw everything, including how divination works.

Her vision of the ruined town had also shown her something else. Scrawled in paint on a piece of tangled metal siding: NEED HELP FINDING MOTHER'S ASHES. She recognized the script as her daughter's, her daughter not yet born at the time of her vision, but she made the likely assumption. Which is why she said one day to Preacher after a particularly riveting scriptural study session, How clever. How clever to reveal the secret by performing it.

Praise be, Preacher said.
Praise to all things that, of their own accord, spell themselves backwards.

THE TRUE STORY of Cain and Abel goes like this: Cain looked down and Abel up. Cain worshipped earth because of its possibilities and Abel the sky because it proved space, which could chart a man walking through a field. Cain never liked a suit, Abel loved a suit with a matching hat. Despite these differences and at any rate, the revelation as revealed by the secret scriptures says that a Great Wheel split the body of Yahweh, which is what made the brothers, the flesh representatives of the concept of the number 2. In the bowels of 2, at the birth moment, everything split-doubled into its most extreme possibilities. This is what the two brothers were.

When the brothers first faced one another, a mirror materialized between them. Mirrors rearrange space and this one was no different and even much more so. This mirror revealed the impossible space between the brothers by which they were 1 and also always 2. They could see their own births and deaths at the same time and in all directions.

Well this was just fine. The problems came along when the mirror shattered. In response, the world organized itself around the atrophied forms of the brothers and then everything lined up and took a turn on the diving board, landing in either one swimming pool or the other.

Let me ask right now, while you are waiting in line for your turn to jump, what would it take for you to invite into your waiting the decategorizing hand of the Lord; what would it take, think about it, what do you think it would take? What would it take to come into the light of not-knowing? Come into the light. Come become hereaftered.

A woman goes to her mailbox. She is hoping for something, anything, from her lover. She never hears from him anymore, though she writes to him.

The children grew up in an instant. It had been a bad year for roses, but a good year for camellias. X's death had been unexpected but quick, a mercy; the university had thrown a nice affair, perhaps she would go to Spain.

She had so many thoughts in a day she would make lists of things to remember to tell him. She found such a list once in the back of her desk drawer, over two decades old:

1. Read everything Freud wrote
2. Become a Girl Scout leader
3. "Hell would like to apologize for this supermarket"

She put this list on the list of things to tell him.

Walking to the mailbox, she observed the light, a late-August light, a golden that edges, and it reminded her of when they met, how when she woke, she would tell him her dreams. It was during a time in which her dreaming life had been extraordinary and vivid. Little did she know how deeply a person could love, how a person could and could not have the object of their love. Which is why they began, years ago, to write to one another at his suggestion.

When she reached the mailbox, she was surprised that there was indeed something: a postcard. A shiny picture of her state capitol. She turned it over to see what was written there. *Open your eyes,* it said. *Now.*

Her eyes were wide open.

A thin coating of the ashy dust that coated everything also coated her on the hell-hot slab.

She was beautiful, Preacher thought, but not in the normal ways. Her beauty was the kind that didn't make a good picture because it moved so fast. He touched her hair. You could use a proper combing, he said. My hair is the story of how I got my name, she replied. Her gaze was unhooked, milky. He had a knack for knowing the words that were last caught in the mouth of a person.

Preacher brought his hands slow and close to the woman's face until his fingertips could feel the ends of her eyelashes and he closed her eyes for good.

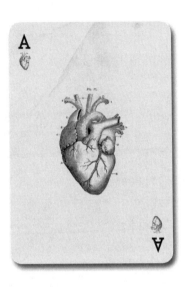

When she was brave enough, the girl Harriet turned over the remaining card on Madam Surget's makeshift table.

Something comes to an end, Madam Surget said. This is a gate card, the heart's path, but broken open, diaspora.

It is the story of people leaving their homes and never coming back. And the moon goes through all its phases at once.

It is what it is. The best you can do is accept it.

Make an offering for what is lost without judging how that offering is received. Always set a place at your table for the dead. Know too that their number includes you. Cast yourself as a figure, leaving. While you go, tell yourself stories you learned and made. It all enters memory, the watery grave of what you will, in other words, forget.

When you can, give the precious version, yourself as you are, the story of your survival after the death created through having loved.

There isn't time to pack a bag, you must be on your way.

THE END

NOTES

TIGER GOES TO THE DOGS

I have read two novels that feature dogs as metaphorical themes: *The Dogs: A Modern Bestiary* by Rebecca Brown (City Lights, 2001) and *Wild Dogs: A Novel* by Helen Humphreys (W.W. Norton & Company, 2006).

TIGER HAS A DEVIL OF A TIME

Though my account of the Harpe brothers has been, in places, fictionalized, it is indebted to the research of regional historians who offer varied, often contradictory, and fascinating accounts of the lives and crimes of the notorious brothers.

TIGER TAKES REGIONAL FAVORITES TO NEW HEIGHTS

"When the Saints Go Marching In": lyrics by Luther Presley and music by Virgil Stamps.

Popularized by Louis Armstrong in the 1930s, the song is traditionally sung during funeral marches. While accompanying the coffin to the graveyard, it is played as a dirge. Upon leaving, it is performed in Southern Dixieland style.

TIGER HITS SHUFFLE

This chapter is an excerpt from the project *Other People's Stories*. Originally commissioned and composed as part of an essay on grief and language, I asked friends to submit a paragraph (or so) length story on any topic of their choosing, from the innocuous to the profound. I am grateful to the friends and family whose stories appear in these pages, and, as much as possible, I tried to preserve their original syntax. Thank you to Anna Saterstrom, Emily Kate Harrison, Kelly Corbin, Guenevere Seastrom, Noah Eli Gordon, Richard Grant, and Elizabeth Frankie Rollins.

TIGER, AS MISS MISSISSIPPI, FAILS TO SAVE CHILDREN OR EXPLAIN
    CANADIAN HISTORY, AND FURTHERMORE CONFUSES "WHOLE"
    WITH "HOLE"

What need is there to weep over parts? The whole of it calls for tears.

Attributed to Lucius Annaeus Seneca.

The Chekhov quote is from a letter written to Aleksandr Semenovich (pseudonym of A. S. Gruzinsky), November 1, 1889.

TIGER DRAWS SOME REBEL FLAGS

Original drawings by Sommer Browning.

ACKNOWLEDGMENTS

Thank you to my Mississippi Gulf Coast and Louisiana family and friends, who, along with many strangers, shared their stories with me during and after Hurricane Katrina.

For their consistent generosities, with great affection, thanks to HR Hegnauer, Christian Peet, Brian Kiteley, Sara Veglahn, Bo McGuire, Erin Cox, Michelle Aldredge, Karla Heeps, Laura Davenport, Helen Humphreys, Tama Baldwin, Meg Harders, Michelle Puckett, Kate Sullivan, Michelle Puckett, Noah Eli Gordon, Eléna Rivera, Max Regan, Mindy Gates, Ellen Orleans, Lisa Birman, Micheline Aharonian Marcom, Gleason Bauer, Diane Kimmell, Sommer Browning, and Eleni Sikelianos. Thanks to Cat Yronwode and Lou Florez for their tireless dedication to Southern Rootwork education. Big love to Lou, who was a tremendous inspiriation throughout the writing of this project and Preacher's character, in particular. With gratitude to my family, especially Karen Redhead, Bill Corbin, Riley Ann Corbin, and George and Annie Haymans.

I am grateful to my colleagues and students at the University of Denver and the Naropa University Summer Writing Program. In particular, thank you, Anne Waldman, for your support and for extending extraordinary opportunities through which to experience community. Thank you to the students, staff, and faculty of Goddard College's

MFA in Creative Writing program, in particular its director, Paul Selig.

Tremendous thanks to Coffee House Press, especially to my excellent and patient editor, Chris Fischbach. A big thanks to Molly Fuller for her wonderful work and support.

I am indebted to friends who read versions of this project and provided feedback and encouragement. Thank you, as ever, Laird Hunt. Also thanks to Dawn Paul, Greg Howard, Mathias Svalina, Adam Dunham, Elizabeth Frankie Rollins, Roger Green, and Bin Ramke.

Casa Libre en la Solana provided several residencies, which afforded me time and space in which to work. Thank you to the Casa Libre community and to Casa Libre's executive director, Kristen Nelson. Thanks to Noah Saterstrom for the ways he was a part of this project. Thank you to Eric Baus for helping disperse the ashes. This project would not have endured without Emily K. Harrison, the reincarnation of Alexandra Romanov. Her vision of this work, staged and deeply felt, has been a gift. Thank you for everything, Jennifer Denrow.

A special thanks to my darling sister, Kelly Corbin, an early and consistent influence who knows how to tell a story, like the one about the Rapture she wrote when we were kids, the very same I read for show-and-tell in grade school, which scared the living hell out of everyone, especially the teacher, much to our entire family's delight.

I would be terribly remiss if I didn't thank cultural icon Barbara Walters, an inspiration to girls and women everywhere.

People died during the writing of this book,
then became a part of it.

RIP Allan, Charles, Ray, Joni, Todd, Karen, Steve, Carol, Ann, Hugh, and Akilah.

FUNDER ACKNOWLEDGMENTS

Coffee House Press is an independent, nonprofit literary publisher. All of our books, including the one in your hands, are made possible through the generous support of grants and donations from corporate giving programs, state and federal support, family foundations, and the many individuals that believe in the transformational power of literature.

This activity is made possible by the voters of Minnesota through a Minnesota State Arts Board Operating Support grant, thanks to a legislative appropriation from the arts and cultural heritage fund. We also receive major operating support from Amazon, the Bush Foundation, the McKnight Foundation, and Target. Our publishing program is supported in part by the Jerome Foundation and an award from the National Endowment for the Arts. To find out more about how NEA grants impact individuals and communities, visit www.arts.gov.

Coffee House Press receives additional support from many anonymous donors; the Alexander Family Fund; Suzanne Allen; the Elmer L. & Eleanor J. Andersen Foundation; the David & Mary Anderson Family Foundation; Patricia Beithon, Bill Berkson & Connie Lewallen; the E. Thomas Binger & Rebecca Rand Fund of the Minneapolis Foundation; the Archer Bondarenko Munificence Fund; the Patrick & Aimee Butler Family Foundation; the Buuck

Family Foundation; the Carolyn Foundation; Claire Casey; Louise Copeland; Jane Dalrymple-Hollo; the Dorsey & Whitney Foundation; Mary Ebert & Paul Stembler; Chris Fischbach & Katie Dublinski; Katharine Freeman; Sally French; Jocelyn Hale & Glenn Miller; Jeffrey Hom; Kenneth & Susan Kahn; the Kenneth Koch Literary Estate; Stephen & Isabel Keating; Allan & Cinda Kornblum; Leslie Larson Maheras; the Lenfestey Family Foundation; Sarah Lutman & Rob Rudolph; Carol & Aaron Mack; George Mack; Joshua Mack; Gillian McCain; Mary & Malcolm McDermid; the Mead Witter Foundation; Sjur Midness & Briar Andresen; Peter Nelson & Jennifer Swenson; the Penguin Group; Marc Porter & James Hennessy; the Rehael Fund-Roger Hale & Nor Hall of the Minneapolis Foundation; the Schwab Charitable Fund; Schwegman, Lundberg & Woessner, P.A.; Jeffrey Sugerman & Sarah Schultz; Nan Swid; Patricia Tilton; the Private Client Reserve of US Bank; VSA Minnesota for the Metropolitan Regional Arts Council; the Archie D. & Bertha H. Walker Foundation; the Wells Fargo Foundation of Minnesota; Stu Wilson & Melissa Barker; the Woessner Freeman Family Foundation; and Margaret & Angus Wurtele.

THE McKNIGHT FOUNDATION

Coffee House Press is an internationally renowned independent book publisher and arts nonprofit based in Minneapolis, MN; through their literary publications and Books in Action program, CHP acts as a catalyst and connector—between authors and readers, ideas and resources, creativity and community, inspiration and action.